Penguin Critical Studies

Great Expectations

Douglas Brooks-Davies is Senior Lecturer in English Literature at the University of Manchester. He read English at Brasenose College, Oxford, and gained his PhD from the University of Liverpool. He lectured in the School of English at the University of Leeds from 1967–70 and has taught at Manchester since then. He has made numerous contributions to scholarly journals and his books include *Number and Pattern in the Eighteenth-Century Novel* (1973), *Spenser's 'Faerie Queene': A Critical Commentary on Books I and II* (1977), *The Mercurian Monarch* (1983), *Pope's 'Dunciad' and the Queen of Night* (1985), *Fielding, Dickens, Gosse, Iris Murdoch and Oedipal 'Hamlet'* (1989), and editions of some of Fielding's novels and of Spenser's *Faerie Queene, Books I to III* (1987). He is General Editor of Manchester University Press's 'Literature in Context' series.

Penguin Critical Studies
Joint Advisory Editors:
Stephen Coote and Bryan Loughrey

Charles Dickens

Great Expectations

Douglas Brooks-Davies

Penguin Books

PENGUIN BOOKS

Published by the Penguin Group
Penguin Books Ltd, 27 Wrights Lane, London W8 5TZ, England
Penguin Books USA Inc., 375 Hudson Street, New York, New York 10014, USA
Penguin Books Australia Ltd, Ringwood, Victoria, Australia
Penguin Books Canada Ltd, 10 Alcorn Avenue, Toronto, Ontario, Canada M4V 3B2
Penguin Books (NZ) Ltd, 182–190 Wairau Road, Auckland 10, New Zealand

Penguin Books Ltd, Registered Offices: Harmondsworth, Middlesex, England

First published 1989
10 9 8 7 6 5

Printed in England by Clays Ltd, St Ives plc
Filmset in 9/11 Monophoto Times

For Peter Howe

But if here you do what is to be done you see how
the same God's in everything.

Contents

Preface   1

Introduction   4
1. Autobiography   4
2. Pip's Journey by Instalments and by Stages   8

Stage 1   *CHAPTERS 1–19*   15
1. In the Beginning: The Primal Pair   16
2. Another Pair: Cain and Abel   24
3. Inset: *George Barnwell* and Pip the Apprentice (chapter 15)   32
4. More Biblical Textures   37
   (a) Adamic Labour and Gentility   37
   (b) Penitence and Penitentiaries   38
   (c) Arks   41
   (d) Christmas and the Pigs   44
5. Retrospect on Stage 1   47

Stage 2   *CHAPTERS 20–39*   55
1. London   56
2. The Ghost of Barnard (chapters 21–22)   61
3. Inset: The Story of Miss Havisham (chapter 22)   64
4. Pip's Adopted Family: Pockets Full of Secrets (see chapter 29)   67
5. Yet More Pairs: Wemmick and the Aged P.; Jaggers and Molly (chapters 25, 26)   70
6. Joe's Journey and Pip's Return (chapters 27–30)   73
7. *Hamlet* at the Centre (chapter 31)   78
8. From *Hamlet* back to Satis (chapters 32–38)   82
9. Magwitch's Return (chapters 39–40)   88

Stage 3   *CHAPTERS 40–59*   **95**
1. *Frankenstein* and the Zombie (chapter 40)   96
2. Magwitch's Story (chapter 42)   102
3. The End of Miss Havisham (chapters 43–44, 49)   108
4. The End of Magwitch (chapters 46–47, 52–56)   111
5. Pip's Return Journey and the Two Endings (chapters 57–59) 118

Conclusion   123

Appendix: Pip's Letter   128

Notes   129

Preface

What I have tried to offer in the following pages is a straightforward yet provocative reading of *Great Expectations* that attempts, without jargon, to be true to what I regard as Dickens's conscious and unconscious intentions and to embrace as wide a range of alternative viewpoints as possible. It is designed to be read on its own terms, without reference to any literary theoretical background, as a companion to the text itself.

My overall approach, however, derives from my sense of the autobiographical status of *Great Expectations* and the importance of recognizing the psychologically revelatory nature of Dickens's text. This being the case, it is worth reminding ourselves of some of the features of Dickens's early life that are relevant to the fictional life of Pip. Dickens was born, and spent his early years, in Portsmouth. When he was five, in 1817, his family moved to Chatham and to the north Kent landscape that lies at the heart of *Great Expectations*. It is no accident that Dickens returned to Chatham before writing the novel, revisiting scenes to provoke memories and aid by sight, sound, smell and touch that mysterious process by which memory is metamorphosed into fiction. At Chatham Dockyard, on St Clement's day (23 November), Dickens heard the blacksmiths process and sing the song in honour of their patron saint that he was to put, many years later, into the mouth of Joe Gargery (*Great Expectations*, chapter 12). From Chatham, Dickens's father, John, would sometimes walk his son to Rochester where, in *Great Expectations*, Miss Havisham's Satis House was to be located; and it was in Chatham that his nursemaid, Mary Weller, took him to a greengrocer's shop where a lodger had given birth to quadruplets, and showed him their dead bodies laid out, side by side, on the top of a chest of drawers. The young Dickens thought there were five babies, not four, and that they looked like pigs' trotters on display in a tripe shop. Here, surely, we have a clue to the opening of *Great Expectations*, with the five dead little Pirrips 'arranged in a neat row'; and a clue, too, to the pig symbolism that proliferates in this as in no other Dickens novel (see Stage 1, section 4 (d) below).

Great Expectations is set also in London, where Dickens lived until shortly before he began the novel. The London of *Great*

1

Expectations is, though, strangely criminal, dark, tainted and 'other'. Why? An answer (there is never one answer, of course, and the answers we do give as critics are always in the end guesses) seems to lie in a secret of Dickens's later childhood, his brief period in Warren's Blacking warehouse. The family had moved again, to Camden Town, in 1822. Increasing money difficulties caused by John Dickens's financial incompetence led to the young Dickens being sent to work, on 9 February 1824, two days after his twelfth birthday, in the boot-blacking warehouse in the Strand, where he was required to wrap and label jars of the product for six shillings (thirty new pence) per week. Dickens was not only lonely and uprooted at the warehouse; he was outraged and humiliated by his parents' refusal to see in him a boy of refined sensibility, vulnerable and intellectually precocious, to whom this kind of indignity should not happen.

Dickens suppressed this episode for much of his adult life, acknowledging it only in his fiction, where his friends, wife and children failed, as they were expected to, to read the emotional distress signals that were being set off. It is mentioned in *Sketches by Boz* and *Pickwick Papers*; it is relived in Oliver Twist's birth in the workhouse and his subsequent employment by Fagin; and it is revisited in considerable detail in David Copperfield's degradation as 'a little labouring hind' in Murdstone and Grinby's warehouse which is situated, like Warren's Blacking, by the river (*David Copperfield*, chapter 11). It is revisited too, I think, in *Great Expectations* when the 'stupid, clumsy labouring-boy' Pip (chapter 8) goes to London to escape the indignities of smithy work only to find himself increasingly implicated in substrate after substrate of crime and deprivation, which seems to make his London experience an extended symbolic brooding on the taint first encountered by Dickens himself in the decaying warehouse occupied by Warren's aptly named Blacking.

I shall return to all this in the main part of the book. For those readers interested in my critical premises, however, I should say that the work of Freud, particularly in relation to the Oedipus complex, has informed some of my attitudes and guided some of my thinking, as indeed it has the work of several of Dickens's most recent American critics. Like them, too, I see Freud's concept of the uncanny (in his essay of that name, reprinted in the *Standard Edition of the Complete Psychological Works of Sigmund Freud*, ed. James Strachey, Anna Freud, *et al.*, vol. 17) as a means of understanding one aspect at least of the ghostly as it infuses *Great Expectations* and Dickens's other late novels. To those wishing to follow me in these and related directions (feminist discourse, deconstructionism, and so on) I recommend Terry Eagleton's *Literary Theory: An Introduction* (Oxford: Basil Blackwell, 1983) as a sound and stimulating starting-point. And for those wishing to relate what I say to recent criticism of Dickens, I have appended brief notes at the end of the book naming the works which I have found most useful.

All *Great Expectations* quotations are from the edition by Angus Calder for Penguin Classics (Harmondsworth: Penguin, 1965).

The quotation in the Dedication is from Peter Howe's *Recollections of the Bhagavad Gita*, poem xviii, in his collection *Origins* (Chatto and Windus: The Hogarth Press, 1981), with the permission of the publishers.

I should like to thank the many students who have talked about *Great Expectations* with me over many years and deepened my understanding of its richness, puzzles, complexity and humour. My special thanks, though, must go to Mary Nixson, without whose insight and presence this book would undoubtedly have remained unwritten.

Douglas Brooks-Davies
June 1988
University of Manchester

Introduction

1. AUTOBIOGRAPHY

Pip's story, narrated by the middle-aged man in his own, autobiographical voice with reticent good humour and a certain amount of ironic self-awareness, is a remarkably compressed and simple one. It has none of the multiple plotting of *Bleak House* (1852–3) or *Our Mutual Friend* (1864–5) to divert attention from the single-mindedness of the narrative, and it reveals little awareness of events that are external to Pip's personal history. Whereas its immediate predecessor, *A Tale of Two Cities* (1859), focused on the French Revolution as an image of contemporary problems and concerns, and *Bleak House* had exposed with satiric fury the outrages perpetuated by a fossilized legal bureaucracy and a petrified aristocracy, *Great Expectations* looks largely at the inner life. Indeed, it is not going too far to say that it is in many ways not so much Pip's autobiography as a version of Dickens's own.

This at least is what Dickens himself seemed to suggest when he wrote to his long-standing friend and biographer John Forster about the novel he began writing in the autumn of 1860:

> The book will be written in the first person throughout, and during these first three weekly numbers you will find the hero to be a boy-child, like David. Then he will be an apprentice ... I have put a child and a good-natured foolish man, in relations that seem to me very funny. Of course I have got in the pivot on which the story will turn too – and which indeed, as you remember, was the grotesque tragi-comic conception that first encouraged me. To be quite sure I had fallen into no unconscious repetitions, I read *David Copperfield* again the other day, and was affected by it to a degree you would hardly believe.

David Copperfield (1849–50) is the most explicitly autobiographical of Dickens's novels. It had exposed to public view in the guise of fiction the unforgettable episode when he had laboured in Warren's Blacking warehouse in order to help his family pay off the debts for which his father was about to be arrested and imprisoned in the Marshalsea; it had celebrated that same father's optimistic foolishness in the shape of Mr Micawber; it had relived his youthful days as a parliamentary reporter and stenographer, and so on.

4

Yet, although *David Copperfield* is built upon images of loss, as *Great Expectations* is from its very first page when Pip stands in the churchyard and realizes that his whole family, apart from himself and Mrs Joe, is dead, its narrator's stance is essentially more extrovert than that of the later novel, his 'I' much less intensely concentrated on himself. Despite the deaths of David's father, mother, and Dora, and the break-up of the family in the Yarmouth ark as Daniel Peggotty and Ham stumble off into a darkly post-diluvial world in search of Emily, the narrating David never becomes as preoccupied with himself as Pip is.

One reason for this is that the earlier novel, unlike *Great Expectations*, is full of characters, many of whom seem to possess an exuberant life of their own rather than functioning as shadowy projections of David's deeper anxieties. Another reason might be that the preoccupation with parental loss and orphanhood occupies less space, proportionately, and carries less emotional weight, than it does in *Great Expectations*. Certainly, Mr Murdstone is brutal and appalling, but the difference between David's perception of him and Pip's perception of Magwitch in the opening chapters of *Great Expectations* – violent and threatening yet also pathetic and vulnerable – is rather like the difference between Jane Eyre's impression of Brocklehurst as a black column and Lucy Snowe's infinitely more suggestive and haunting dream figures in *Villette*. Murdstone, like Magwitch, is an image of the hated aspect of the father seen as authoritarian threat, but there is little doubt that Magwitch is closer to the dark world of Dickens's unconscious mind. The demanding aspect of Magwitch is, as it were, Dickens's father John in his role of constantly impecunious and demanding beggar, dunning his son for everything he can get from him. Now that his father has been dead for ten years, Dickens's creative self returns to him, grotesquely enlarges his intolerable characteristics, yet muses on him elegiacally, too, seeing the pity of him and feeling what an inextricable part of Dickens's own personality he has become. The difference between Murdstone and Magwitch can, then, be simply explained by the fact that when Murdstone was invented John Dickens was still alive, and when Magwitch leaped out from among the tombstones into Dickens's mind he was dead.

At this point it is useful to recall the phrase 'unconscious repetitions' from the letter quoted above. Although the word 'unconscious' did not possess its modern psychoanalytic meaning in Dickens's day it could, nevertheless, convey the sense of 'operating below the threshold of consciousness'. As *stories David Copperfield* and *Great Expectations* are extremely unlike each other. In using the phrase Dickens was, I think, trying to convey his awareness that, at root, both novels revisited the indignities he felt he had undergone as a child, his sense that the 'repetitions' were not so much narrative as emotional because David and Pip were both drawn from the same dark reservoir within his unconscious self.

Great Expectations was written in weekly rather than the usual monthly instalments, and was thus the product of intense physical and imaginative pressure, the kind of pressure that inevitably drives the writer down into the depths of his creative being. In those depths Dickens discovered an image of himself in the orphan Pip: a boy who had wanted passionately to escape from the shaming indignity of increasing childhood poverty and an imprisoned and imprisoning father, and who sensed that education offered him a means of escape from the spiral of moneyless degradation into which he felt his father had plunged him.

And if the blacking warehouse itself makes only one incidental explicit appearance in *Great Expectations* (Joe's 'me and Wopsle went off straight to look at the Blacking Ware'us. But we didn't find that it come up to its likeness in the red bills at the shop doors'; chapter 27), a glance at the description of it in the autobiographical fragment that Dickens wrote in 1851 after the death of his father reveals that the idea and image of it haunt the novel. In the fragment it is filthy and rat-infested:

> It was a crazy, tumble-down old house, abutting of course on the river, and literally overrun with rats. Its wainscotted rooms, and its rotten floors and staircase, and the old grey rats swarming down in the cellars . . . and the dirt and decay of the place, rise up visibly before me, as if I were there again.

Even acknowledging the nineteenth-century obsession with such images (as in Tennyson's 'Mariana' and Browning's 'Childe Roland'), we must recognize the peculiar intensity of Dickens's preoccupation with the landscape of decay in *Great Expectations*. It had, of course, appeared in his other novels. But whereas in *Bleak House*, for example, it says something about the appalling conditions of the urban poor, in *Great Expectations* it talks of Pip's and Dickens's sense of his contaminated childhood self. The blacksmith's boy who manages to wish away his demanding Magwitch of a father, imagine into being a wealthy fairy godmother, and turns into a rather unlovely snob who is always confronted with images of dirt, dereliction and decay (at Satis House, Barnard's Inn, and so forth) registers and revives Dickens the social climber's constant sense of his own contamination by the blacking warehouse. The fact that *Great Expectations* is haunted by convicts and prisons as well suggests the extent to which it, more so than *Little Dorrit* (1855–7) or any of the other novels, reworks and recreates Dickens's most buried childhood grievances. Notice, too, how the north Kent marshes which are Pip's homeland are a version of the landscape of Dickens's happiest childhood memories at Chatham. Pip leaves them and returns to them at the novel's end as Dickens had himself (1857) returned to possess Gad's Hill Place, the exquisite Georgian house which, as a boy, he had gazed at in the company of his father, expressing astonishing disbelief when John Dickens had told him that if he worked very hard he might own it one day.

The house, in which he wrote *Great Expectations*, lies off the Rochester to Gravesend road. The river beyond Gravesend is the scene of Magwitch's death; Satis House is in Rochester, whose cathedral bells toll mournfully at the beginning of chapter 49. Pip's journey to gentility and the stripping away of his genteel trappings and illusions about gentility, image, as in a dreamscape in which everything is skewed and not quite 'right', Dickens's perception of himself, now that he has socially arrived, as a man who is still fighting the ghosts of his childhood and of his father.

Just before he started work on *Great Expectations*, Dickens published a series of essays entitled *The Uncommercial Traveller*. One of these ('Travelling Abroad') narrates a strange hallucinatory experience. The narrator, Dickens, is travelling past Gad's Hill Place as Dickens himself did when a boy with his father, and encounters a 'queer small boy' who is looking at Gad's Hill Place:

'You admire that house?' said I.

'Bless you, sir,' said the very queer small boy, 'when I was not more than half as old as nine, it used to be a treat for me to be brought to look at it. And now I am nine, I come by myself to look at it. And ever since I can recollect, my father, seeing me so fond of it, has often said to me, "If you were to be very persevering and were to work hard, you might some day come to live in it." Though that's impossible!' said the very queer small boy, drawing a low breath, and now staring at the house out of the window with all his might.

I was rather amazed to be told this by the very queer small boy; for that house happens to be *my* house, and I have reason to believe that what he said was true.

If we bear this in mind in conjunction with that sentence in the autobiographical fragment when he ponders the degradation of the blacking warehouse days and writes that 'even now, famous and caressed and happy, I often forget in my dreams that I have a dear wife and children; even that I am a man; and wander desolately back to that time of my life', then we have a major clue to one way at least of understanding the Dickens of *Great Expectations*. It is not so much about the rotten inner core of Victorian society, the gaining of money and its advantages through the labour and humiliation of others (though it is of course about these things), as about Dickens's own sense of his need to escape from – and his entrapment by – the past.

The novel is a shaped and meticulously – even brilliantly – crafted fiction that nevertheless reveals in almost every chapter its deep affinities with Dickens's own life. This is not to say that our reading of the novel should be limited by what we know of that life. On the contrary, recognition of this work's buried autobiographical roots expands our critical awareness by revealing to us the astonishing nature of the processes by which mundane detail and psychological traumas are transformed into art. Who would have guessed that the Marshalsea could have produced, all those years later at Gad's Hill Place, the 'marshes' of *Great Expectations*, pronounced 'meshes' by the locals (so as to turn them into emblems of entrapment), across which lie the prison ships where Magwitch is incarcerated (end of chapter 2)? Who would have guessed that from these marshes the whole novel would have developed, as from some primeval, secret-hugging, swamp?

2. PIP'S JOURNEY BY INSTALMENTS AND BY STAGES

Great Expectations begins in a churchyard and returns to that same churchyard in the final chapter with Pip placing the image of his young self in the form of Joe's and Biddy's son Pip – 'I again!' – 'on a certain tombstone' from which he points to the parental graves on which Pip the elder had meditated so hard in chapter 1 (a comparison with Dickens's encounter with himself as 'the very queer small boy' is inevitable).

The novel's structure is thus circular: a fact readily apparent to us as readers of a modern one-volume text, as also to readers of the three-volume edition of October 1861, but one that the weekly serialization of *Great Expectations* in Dickens's recently founded periodical *All The Year Round* from 1 December 1860 to 3 August 1861 concealed. Its weekly readers, whatever Dickens's overall plan for the novel's plot, encountered a growing and developing story. They could write to its author and hope to change or influence the narrative. They could affect authorial strategies by doing the most dreaded thing of all, withholding their money; for when sales fall off a serial novelist knows that he is failing his public. For the weekly readers, therefore, Dickens devised smaller-scale structures, often based on the best-seller technique of mystification. One of *Great Expectations*'s early reviewers, Edwin Whipple, commented on how successful Dickens had been in this respect when he wrote that he had read this novel

as we have read all Mr Dickens's previous works, as it appeared in instalments, and can testify to the felicity with which expectation was excited and prolonged, and to the series of surprises which accompanied the unfolding of the plot of the story. (*Atlantic Monthly*, September 1861)

As well as suspense, surprise and mystification, however, Dickens developed a technique of *thematic repetitions* between the endings of the weekly parts. Normally a serial episode comprised a two-chapter module; but that depended on the length of the chapters involved, and so occasionally an instalment consisted of one long chapter, as in the cases of chapters 5 and 8. The Penguin edition marks the end of each instalment with an asterisk, thereby making it easy to see, for instance, how the conclusion of instalment 1's stolen pie and file and Pip's stealthy escape from the house on to the marshes (end of chapter 2) are relived in the ending of instalment 2 (end of chapter 4) with the pork pie's loss about to be discovered and Pip fleeing in terror only to run 'head foremost' at the house door into a group of soldiers, one of whom offers him a pair of handcuffs.

The handcuffs suggest Pip's feeling of guilt over the theft and mark his acquisition of an equivalent of Magwitch's leg-irons, which are the reason he stole the file in the first place. The means of liberating Magwitch (the file) thus symbolically binds Pip to him, as the soldiers announce by bringing the handcuffs and then (opening sentence of chapter 5, beginning of instalment 3), by a pun which opens up vistas of surreality, turning into a file themselves: 'The apparition of a file of soldiers . . .'.

Another metamorphosis of the handcuffs occurs at the close of instalment 3 (end of chapter 5) where the logic of repetitive structuring turns them into the 'massive rusty chains' of the prison ship which no file can saw through. But note that the file, Joe's file, is reintroduced by the stranger in chapter 10 and 'haunts' Pip at chapter 10's close: 'I was haunted by the file too. A dread possessed me that . . . [it] would reappear . . . in my sleep I saw the file coming at me out of a door'. (The end of chapter 10 also marks the end of instalment 6.)

Meanwhile, at the end of chapter 5 and of instalment 3, Magwitch relieves Pip of guilt over the pie by saying that he stole it himself, thus once more answering the end of instalment 1.

Again at the end of instalment 3, as the two convicts are received into the prison ship 'the ends of the torches were flung hissing into the water, and went out, as if it were all over with [Magwitch]'. This is an image of Magwitch's death and of Pip's and society's willingness to erase all memory of him. As such it anticipates the end of instalment 4 (last paragraph of chapter 7) when it is again night and Pip leaves Joe for the first time and the stars – themselves symbolic anticipations of chilly and remote Estella ('the star') in the next instalment (chapter 8) – twinkle but 'without throwing any light on' Pip's various mental queries about the visit to Miss Havisham he is just setting out on. The extinguished torches 'become' non-illumining stars by the same structural and imaginative logic that turned the file into the ghostly apparition of a row of soldiers and the handcuffs into massive rusty mooring chains. And the equation of torches with stars makes Pip's journey to Estella a farewell to Joe that parallels the relegation of Magwitch to the deathly blackness of the Hulks: Magwitch and Joe merge symbolically as Pip begins his progress to gentility.

The Penguin text's asterisks enable any reader to pursue the kind of enquiry I have begun here. What the parallels and metamorphoses of one image into another reveal in the end, though, is that repetition is fundamental to the meaning of the narrative. The repetitions tell us that Pip's narrative is actually *about* repetition; that it is about a man whose imaginative life is dominated by a small number of obsessive images and concerns, most, if not all, of which derive from his preoccupation with himself as an orphan. This preoccupation turns him into a man who insistently recreates images of parents and the loss of parents in almost every direction he turns.

Repetition even undermines the sense of movement fostered by Pip's journey to London to establish himself as a gentleman. Not only is the end of that journey marked by Magwitch's return as Pip's 'second father' (chapter 39); its beginning in chapters 20 and

21 confronts Pip with two plaster death-masks in Jaggers's office that are somewhat reminiscent in their twoness and criminality of the two convicts who struggled in the ditch in chapter 5. It also confronts him, in Barnard's Inn, the site of his first London lodgings, with a grisly cemetery of a wasteland that combines chapter 1's churchyard with the overgrown wilderness of Satis House. Barnard's Inn turns out in addition to be inhabited by Herbert Pocket, the 'pale young gentleman' of Satis House (chapter 11).

If it is a fact that in these and other details Dickens's serial (the noun was, according to the *Oxford English Dictionary*, first used with reference to a Dickens novel) proceeds not so much serially as through repetitive echoes, instalments that have as their goal the Magwitch and churchyard of the beginning, it is nevertheless also a fact that the book version, particularly in its three-volume form, contributes to the illusion that Pip actually progresses, and that he does so in three distinct *stages*, one for each of the three volumes of the original publication in book format: volume 1, chapters 1–19, at the end of which we reach the conclusion of 'the first stage of Pip's expectations'; volume 2, chapters 20–39, at the end of which we have reached 'the end of the second stage of Pip's expectations'; and volume 3, chapters 40–59, at the end of which we are, perhaps significantly, told nothing at all.

The word *stage* is wonderfully ambiguous, exactly right for Pip's journey that is really no journey. It suggests three things: the *sections of a journey* as undertaken by a stage-coach (but in this connection *stage* was often used to refer not so much to the journey as to the stopping places that divided the journey into its several stages); the *site of a dramatic presentation* (that platform within the circumscribed limits of which players act out their roles); and the *gallows* (*stage* as 'a scaffold for execution', as the *Oxford English Dictionary* defines it).

Does Dickens mean us to infer these three levels of meaning from Pip's narrative, gathering as we do so that it is about a journey by stops rather than starts involving the acting out of a part that is fixated on death, and especially death by hanging? I am sure that he does. Consider the pirate hanged from the gibbet (end of chapter 1), Miss Havisham 'hanging ... by the neck' (end of chapter 8), and Magwitch's conviction that he 'should of a certainty be hanged if took' at the end of chapter 39, just at the conclusion of 'the second *stage* of Pip's expectations'. Then consider the way play-acting is used as a theme in the novel to underline the hollowness of Pip's

11

gentility. Each stage of the novel, in fact, sees Pip either acting or learning to act, from the moment when he wonders why he 'was going to play at Miss Havisham's, and what on earth [he] was expected to play at' (chapter 7) and Miss Havisham utters her teasingly ambiguous, 'I have a sick fancy that I want to see some play' (chapter 8).

Moreover, each of the three stages finds Pip shadowed by the figure of Wopsle, whose increasing failure to take the London stage by storm comments on Pip's own failure as an actor in the drama of urbane gentility. More precisely than that, in each stage Wopsle performs before Pip a play which relates in a more or less obvious way to Pip's situation, functioning like one of those microcosmic mirrors in a Van Eyck painting, or like *Hamlet*'s play within the play. The first of these is the eighteenth-century playwright George Lillo's *The London Merchant; or, the History of George Barnwell* (1731), still popular on the nineteenth-century stage, a reading of which Wopsle compels Pip to attend in chapter 15; the second is *Hamlet* itself (chapter 31, but attended and described by Joe earlier, in chapter 27); the third is an unnamed play with accompanying pantomime in chapter 47 (on each of these, see below, pp. 32–6, 78– 81, 111–13).

Finally, just as the instalment endings sustain a repetitively chiming dialogue with each other in the manner noted above, so do the final paragraphs of each of the three stages have an echoic relationship.

At the end of stage 1 'the mists had all solemnly risen now, and the world lay spread before' Pip as he rides on his way to London (chapter 19); at the end of stage 3 in its published form (see below, pp. 120–22, on the novel's two endings), Pip takes Estella's hand 'and, as the morning mists had risen long ago when I first left the forge, so, the evening mists were rising now' (chapter 59); while at the end of stage 2, in contrast, after Magwitch's return (chapter 39) 'the clocks of the Eastward churches were striking five, the candles were wasted out, the fire was dead, and the wind and rain intensified the thick black darkness'.

Two paragraphs concluding with rising mists frame a paragraph that ends in darkness. Rising mists suggest optimism, however unjustified it may turn out to be; thick rain and misty blackness are images of the deepest despair.

What is perhaps less immediately obvious is the way each of these stage endings is rooted in the last lines of Milton's *Paradise Lost*, the moment when Adam and Eve are finally expelled from Eden after the Fall:

> They looking back, all the eastern side beheld
> Of Paradise, so late their happy seat,
> Waved over by that flaming brand, the gate
> With dreadful faces thronged and fiery arms:
> Some natural tears they dropped, but wiped them soon;
> The world was all before them, where to choose
> Their place of rest, and providence their guide:
> They hand in hand with wandering steps and slow,
> Through Eden took their solitary way.
>
> (Book 12, lines 641–9)

Pip's 'the world lay spread before me' is clearly Miltonic (line 646 of the above passage) rather than a reminiscence of Wordsworth's recollection of the line at the opening of *The Prelude*, Book 1 as he revisits the maternal landscape of his childhood ('escaped/From the vast city, where I long had pined/A discontented sojourner: now free,/... The earth is all before me').

What the Miltonic echo tells us (for it works as an *allusion* rather than as an incidental or coincidental borrowing) is that *Great Expectations*, like *Paradise Lost*, is a narrative about loss – primal loss – and about a subsequent existence devoted to ways of coping with that loss. Milton's poem is built on the Christian myth and the idea of paradise restored through the second Adam, Christ. *Great Expectations*, despite the appearance of Christian symbolism in it, is psychologically rather than theologically oriented. It confronts us and it leaves us with a solitary Pip who is still the victim of the parental loss that he understood to be fundamental to his character and perceptions of things in the churchyard on that Christmas Eve all those years ago in chapter 1. There is no Saviour for Pip. The world that lies spread before *him* turns out to be filthy with London grime and decay, haunted by Magwitch and by Pip's obsessive returns to Satis with its buried old woman and her adopted daughter.

It is possible, I think, to argue that *Paradise Lost* has an even more precise significance than this for Dickens's novel. For Wordsworth, in *The Prelude*, childhood is equated with imaginative and personal liberty. If he can return to childhood (literally by visiting the landscape of his boyhood, imaginatively by remembering and writing about it), his Eden is recaptured. In *Great Expectations*, however, Dickens produces for Pip a spread-out world that is

13

repetitively inscribed with reminders of the loss of his parents: death-masks, Barnard's Inn as burial ground, and so on. How does this relate to *Paradise Lost*? By suggesting that Pip's desolate world, built as it is on the loss of father and mother, is somehow a fallen world minus its Adam and Eve. Horrified at their absence, Pip has to reinvent them. Magwitch is thus brought into being as a fallen Adam inhabiting a marshy wilderness; and Miss Havisham is Pip's fascinated resurrection of Mother Eve, dwelling within the even more desolate wilderness of Satis House and its grounds.

Pip's attempt to link with Estella is therefore, on this level, an attempt to duplicate the marriage between his own parents perceived as an image of Edenic happiness. That much the published ending of the novel tells us with its echo of the ending of stage 1 (the rising mists) and its holding of hands ('I took her hand in mine, and we went out of the ruined place'; compare Adam and Eve 'hand in hand'). But for Pip, as I argue later, it can only be an image, can only be imagined, not achieved. Pip never overcomes the loss of his parents sufficiently to have a life of his own. He is always an exile without a mate because he is haunted by his parents as a lost, disowned, and dead Adam and Eve.

Stage 1 CHAPTERS 1–19

1. In the Beginning: The Primal Pair

The first chapter of *Great Expectations* is a beginning that is about Pip's own beginning as, at the age of seven or so, on Christmas Eve (the anniversary of Christianity's beginning) Pip goes to the churchyard to try to establish his identity in relation to his dead mother and father. With no photographs or other portraiture to aid him ('for their days were long before the days of photographs'; chapter 1), Pip imagines his parents from the lettering on their tombstones, visualizing a mother who is 'freckled and sickly' and a father who is 'square, stout, dark ... with curly black hair'. As Pip gazes into the gloom at the marshes and, feeling the full burden of his lonely orphanhood, starts to cry, a 'terrible voice' tells him to be quiet and 'a fearful man, all in coarse grey' appears from among the graves – 'a man who had been soaked in water, and smothered in mud, and lamed by stones, and cut by flints, and stung by nettles, and torn by briars'.

This is his introduction to Magwitch, who will become his 'second father'. The fact that he leaps out from among the graves while Pip is meditating on his dead parents makes him some kind of apparition, even 'the ghost of [Pip's] own father' himself, to quote Joe's words on *Hamlet* in chapter 27.

Magwitch is the dead father (or one aspect of him) imagined back into being and inspiring in Pip the terror that ghosts always have for us. He is the father conceived of as a hated and threatening figure (compare Murdstone in *David Copperfield*), and as such is in absolute contrast to simple, kind and loving Joe (chapter 2). On the most elementary level, Pip's narrative is about Magwitch's appearance, disappearance and return, and Pip's subsequent sympathy and love for him; and about Pip's parallel rejection of – and return to – Joe, with deepened love and respect. Magwitch and Joe are thus twinned and complementary aspects of Pip's vision of the father as an archetype containing threat and authority and love, dignity, and helplessness: an archetype created out of Dickens's perception of his own role as father and memories of John Dickens.

But at the very beginning it is Magwitch, not Joe, who has priority. He is the figure who appears in the churchyard almost like a memory of Pip's real father. Indeed, it is as if Pip is, in this opening chapter, blurring the distinction between the external experience of some kind of threatening ghost and the internal experience of recalling a Murdstone-like memory of his real father from his infant past, until this moment completely forgotten.

Consider in this connection the fact that the whole novel is an act of memory, a recalling by the middle-aged Pip of his childhood and young adulthood, and that this made it for readers in 1860 an *historical* novel. Not only is it set in the days before photographs but in pre-railway days, too, days when you could still get 'fat sweltering one-pound notes' (chapter 10): sovereigns replaced paper notes in 1826 and for the rest of Dickens's life (he was born in 1812 and died in 1870). The narrative is set in the past as a symbolic way of informing us that it is about reaching back into the past, into buried memories. It also tells us that the period of Pip's childhood (pre–1826) is the period of Dickens's own childhood.

These are some of the things suggested by the novel's beginning. As is often the case with acts of critical description, however, my outline has reduced to over-neat formulae the rich and complicated phenomenon it is attempting to portray. What Magwitch 'means' is in the end apparent only from consideration of all the multifarious ways Pip presents him to us, and I would say from the evidence of the fifth paragraph of chapter 1 that Magwitch is not just terrible and a pathetically vulnerable victim but that, as a victim, he is a version of Isaiah's vision of the despised Christ, 'rejected of men; a man of sorrows, and acquainted with grief ... wounded for our transgressions ... bruised for our iniquities ... taken from prison and from judgement' (Isaiah 53:3, 5, 8. Notice, too, how Jaggers constantly washes his hands as Pilate did (e.g. Matthew 27:24)). The implication of this fusion of father with scapegoat is that the hated aspect of the father is being recognized by the remembering narrator as an *unjust* perception, the product of his own prejudices and needs. Pip's father-victim is, in other words, the product of the same psychological and anthropological mechanism that required the scapegoat Christ.

Magwitch as scapegoat is not just a psychological reality for Pip, though. By making him a convict Dickens suggests that mid-nineteenth-century English society needs its criminals as scapegoats, too; so that Magwitch as outcast convict, on society's margins, is a passionate reformist's accusation aimed at a loathsomely complacent social structure and hierarchy. Some of the images through which he is depicted have a Darwinian ring to them, as if to be an outcast is to be reduced to the level of an animal precursor: 'I wish I was a frog. Or a eel!'. Later he eats like a dog, manifesting as he does so the survivor characteristics of suspicion and rapidity:

> The man took strong sharp sudden bites, just like the dog ... and he looked sideways here and there while he ate, as if he thought there was danger in every direction, of somebody's coming to take the pie away. (chapter 3)

It is also difficult to imagine that Pip, whose narrative is shot through with biblical allusions (see section 4, below), is unaware that his Magwitch who leaps out from among the graves is reminiscent of the terrifying Legion in Mark 5, the man who, possessed by 'an unclean spirit', 'had his dwelling among the tombs; and no man could bind him, no, not with chains: Because that he had been often bound with fetters and chains, and the chains had been plucked asunder by him'. Jesus commands the spirits to leave him, and they enter the Gadarene swine. Magwitch, the narrative suggests, is not so easily dealt with. It suggests in addition that possession by devils is a cynically convenient way of labelling and thus dismissing those whom society decides to reject. Dickens's point is that Magwitch is no more Legion than Pip or his readers are. He is outcast, alien and marginal for reasons which are spelled out for us in chapter 42 when Magwitch narrates his autobiography, and which are all too close to those discoverable from the life stories of the underprivileged of our own day for us to feel complacent about them.

Magwitch's name, compounded of Latin *magus* (magician) + witch, indicates that there is something demonically irrepressible about him, that he has a magician's power over Pip's destiny. The description of Miss Havisham as the 'Witch of' Satis (chapter 11) and as *weird* (chapters 8 and 19; the word does not just mean *strange* but *fate-determining*, thus denoting someone who controls another person's destiny) is one way in which Dickens pairs the two, making her the partner to Pip's Magwitch father and so completing Pip's horrified and grotesque recreation of his long-lost parents.

Magwitch leaps out from among graves and Miss Havisham is entombed at Satis, the buried mother revisited. There is no time at Satis (the clocks were all stopped twenty years before) because the dead know no time. When Pip first meets her in chapter 8 he recalls a 'ghastly waxwork' effigy and an excavated skeleton, seeing her as a corpse and her clothes as 'grave-clothes'. And note that one of the first things she says to Pip is, 'You are not afraid of a woman who has never seen the sun since you were born?', which surely means not only, 'I have been concealed in this house the whole of your lifetime' but also, linking as it does Pip with her incarceration, 'I gave birth to you and died in doing so: your birth caused my burial in this tomb'.

Miss Havisham's attire needs comment, too. She wears 'graveclothes', yes, but with flowers in her hair and her dress so disordered that she would have been recognized at the time as a figure of the Ophelia type so beloved of the mid- and late nineteenth century (the best known is Millais' painting of the drowned Ophelia which dates from 1851–2): Ophelia betrayed and driven to madness and suicide by Hamlet; the Ophelia over whose corpse Gertrude says, 'I thought thy bride-bed to have deck'd, sweet maid,/And not t'have strew'd thy grave' (*Hamlet*, V. i). This is particularly relevant in view of Pip's attendance at Wopsle's *Hamlet* in chapter 31.

Equally interesting, however, is the meaning of the Ophelia type from the viewpoint of Victorian sexual politics. Mad Ophelia, garlanded and bridal, was a popular contemporary image of female lunacy. Actresses playing Ophelia were advised to visit asylums in order to study the role in the flesh, as it were; and the evidence seems to suggest that, conversely, some mad women (particularly those accused of 'erotomania', or madness induced by excessive sexual appetite and depravity) were themselves dressed up to look like Ophelia for the benefit of visitors who happened to come equipped with their photographic apparatus (see Elaine Showalter, *The Female Malady: Women, Madness and English Culture, 1830– 1980* (London: Virago, 1985), fig. 17). Dickens himself, after a visit to an asylum in 1851, noted how many more mad women there were than mad men; but without, in this particular essay in *Household Words* at any rate, caring to enquire much further. The notion of madness as something culturally defined and definable is, after all, rather sophisticated and even outrageous. Dickens seems to have thought it was too much for his popular journalism but, after the breakdown of his marriage and formal separation from his wife, Catherine, and the irruption of his passion for Ellen Ternan, he revisited and revised his thoughts about women and madness in *Great Expectations*. For one of the things that Miss Havisham tells us is that Dickens now admits it is *men* who define female madness. Having identified certain women as mad from the viewpoint of established male norms and prejudices, they then imprison them in asylums as Ophelia icons, or whatever other image happens to suit. Miss Havisham is mad Ophelia as the *victim* of male treachery, and as such is an image as strongly feminist as anything in *Villette* or *Jane Eyre*. Miss Havisham as Compeyson's victim stands for all women who have lost their selfhood through being appropriated and betrayed by men (including you, the male reader, me, the male critic, Pip, Dickens . . .). Of course, she need not have shut herself away. But patriarchy has the appalling power, Dickens says, to turn women into helpless victims, to disable them. In this way, too, Miss Havisham is Magwitch's partner. He is outcast and rejected, on the margins of society. So is she. Convict and madwoman: those are the parents that Pip, outsider of an orphan that he is, invents for himself while wishing so very hard that he belonged and that he wasn't just *like* everybody else but better than them: a gentleman, in other words. Which takes us back to Dickens himself, sitting now at Gad's Hill and wondering there, with his father dead, his mother aged and impossible, and his wife gone, whether he has really got anywhere at all in his life.

As far as the plot of *Great Expectations* goes, though, it is the dead-mother aspect of Miss Havisham that is most important. Notice in this connection how, in chapter 11 (Pip's second visit), there is an occurrence of one of Dickens's favourite puns ('this house strikes you old and *grave*, boy'; my italics); and also that one of the attendant relatives 'whose name was Camilla, very much reminded me of my sister', which makes it seem as if Pip, visiting his dead mother in a catacomb, discovers, in a surreally dreamlike way, the image of the sister-mother Mrs Joe who, he feels, has betrayed him so badly and who is now being justly humiliated before the 'real' mother. (The feminists among Dickens's readers will, however, be able to supply a rather different reading of Mrs Joe's put-upon and underprivileged life from the totally subjective one Pip tries to impose on us.)

Above all else, I suppose, Pip's bride of a mother, Miss Havisham, is what Freud was later (but not all that much later) to label 'the mother as object of Oedipal desire': that is, the object of his sexual attention, however suppressed that may be to him. Freud derived his perception from the plot of Sophocles' *Oedipus Rex*, in which Oedipus is revealed to have killed his father and to be married to his mother, Jocasta. According to Freud, whose interpretation of human behaviour is very male, to say the least, all boys want to do exactly this in infancy: obliterate the father and be one with the mother in his place. Applied to Pip, it seems to work: Miss Havisham's bridal status is a wish-fulfilment on Pip's part, a holding of his mother in his imagination as a perpetual virgin, waiting for him, abandoned and thus sexually unassailable by the 'father' Compeyson. At which point we might well ask, how many fathers has Pip got? I suspect the answer is, as many as he imagines he has. Compeyson shares curly hair and physical darkness with the imagined father of the tombstone (chapters 1 and 42); Magwitch, simply because he is so terrifying, is the father as prohibitor, saying 'no' to Pip's desire to slip under those green mounds in the churchyard and be at one with his earth mother Georgiana again (*Georgiana*, as the feminine form of *George*, derives from the Greek word *gē*, or earth. Gē is the earth goddess; the name George means ploughman, labourer on the land). And Jaggers is a prohibiting father, too, when Pip meets him in chapter 11, a dark and mysterious figure who accuses him of unnamed crimes as he makes his way down the stairs from Miss Havisham's room which is also her bedroom.

The Oedipal interpretation links up with Miss Havisham as lunatic Ophelia to suggest that Dickens was feeling his way towards a psychology of male appropriation of the female in terms of Oedipal possession. That is, that the male need to extrude women from society, to dominate and possess yet marginalize them, is seen by Dickens in *Great Expectations* to have its roots in the boy's need to hug his mother to himself, imprisoned forever virginal in the vaults of his memory and imagination. From this point of view, Biddy is a girl and woman who refuses capture by the Oedipal trap: kind and loving towards Pip, she nevertheless rejects his patronage and chooses to remain herself rather than succumbing to his image of her.

Yet again, though, as we try to understand as fully as possible the implications of the extraordinary figure that is Miss Havisham, especially in conjunction with the vision of her young self in the form of Estella, we are driven back to the games the creative mind plays with autobiographical experience. Old and young, forbidding and somehow repellent yet infinitely attractive, she seems to have more than an element of Maria Beadnell about her. Maria was Dickens's first real love, so far as we know, and she spurned him as Estella spurns and taunts Pip. When he met her again many years later (in 1855 after a written correspondence initiated by her that seems to have reawakened all the agony, excitement and longing that he had felt for her when he was in his late teens) she was, he discovered to his horror (but of course biographers of Dickens report only his side of the story), fat, simpering, affected and unattractive. Is Miss Havisham in part his imagination's revenge on Maria for having held her so close as a precious icon of lost perfect love? It seems so. And by the time he was writing *Great Expectations* he was chasing after the young actress Ellen Ternan and not having as much luck as he would have liked; so that she contributes to Estella, too. Finally, what do we make of the fact that when Dickens sold his London home, Tavistock House, to settle fully at Gad's Hill, he burned all his letters and papers of the previous twenty years? This was a couple of months before he started *Great Expectations*. In other words, Dickens broke with his past, eradicating all the precious external signs of treasured memory, and then immediately created a novel in which the narrator *remembers*, and in which there is a figure who refuses to let the past go free. I don't know what to make of that; but simply knowing about it alters my own response to the novel.

Miss Havisham is the past in all its deadness, musty and dark. Although it is impossible to unravel all the strands, she is clearly a deeply personal and multivalent image for Dickens, and it is essential in trying to understand her to remember her virtual inseparability from Estella. The clue that they are 'really' one in Pip's mind is dropped by Pip in chapter 15 and followed up by Joe when he talks of paying a ' "call on Miss Est – Havisham." "Which her name," said Joe, gravely, "ain't Estavisham, Pip, unless she have been rechris'ened." ' The old woman *is* the younger and both are the Eve who could make a paradise of Pip's paradise lost. But the Satis wilderness of a 'rank garden . . . overgrown with tangled weeds' (end of chapter 8) remains a destroyed Eden, the exact complement to the wilderness of the marshes inhabited by Magwitch. If Estella is the unattainable star, I cannot help thinking that Miss Havisham is, literally, Eve; for her name sounds like a reversal of the Hebrew for the *woman* of Genesis 2:23 as commonly transliterated in the nineteenth century: *chavah*. Dickens could have come across this in any dictionary of the Bible.

To try and explain further what I think is going on in Pip's mind as he narrates his tale: at the end of chapter 8 Estella is 'everywhere' in the garden, even 'going out into the sky'. She is the spiritual aspect of Miss Havisham whom at this moment Pip imagines he sees hanging from a beam: Miss Havisham's soul, in fact, rising to heaven. This is in a way the ultimate – even though it is the first – statement of Miss Havisham as the unattainable yet infinitely desired Eve-mother.

But the human mind is an inventive creature, always trying to circumvent the impossible. Estella exists as a possible way of possessing the mother, at once soul or spiritual essence and a version of the mother who is, from the point of view of age, marriageable. The fact that Estella turns out to be Magwitch's daughter and so, because he is Pip's 'second father', Pip's sister, merely confirms the level of incestuous repetition that preoccupies Pip. In chasing after Estella he is imagining himself pursuing his mother (hence Estella always leads him to Miss Havisham or, as at the end, to Satis). Wopsle's recitation of the table of kinship just before Pip returns to Satis in chapter 11 (Wopsle has, after all, 'professional occasion to bear in mind what female relations a man might not marry' (chapter 10)) suggests that Dickens knows exactly what is going on here, as does the detail that Pip was brought up by his sister 'by hand' (that is, she bottle-fed him and she also beat him); for this tells us that even his waking, let alone his unconscious, mind confuses sister with punitive and milk-bestowing images of the mother.

2. Another Pair: Cain and Abel

(NOTE: Magwitch's Christian name is Abel, though we are not told this until chapter 40; and Orlick is referred to as Cain in chapter 15.)

Many nineteenth-century novels are written in a tradition in which the life-history of an individual is presented as his or her spiritual history, its shape being interpreted in accord with certain aspects of biblical history. The hero/heroine is born in sin, his/her birth being in effect a recapitulation of early Genesis; s/he wanders, often an orphan, in exile and error from his/her true home, as the Israelites did, and so forth. It is a particularly Protestant (even Nonconformist) way of reading a life, and the nineteenth century was reminded of it by reading and rereading Bunyan's *Pilgrim's Progress* among other texts. I examine the overall place of biblical symbolism in *Great Expectations* in section 4 below. Here I concentrate on a pattern that is established right at the beginning as a complement to Pip's search for his lost pair of parents, the pattern of Cain and Abel.

When Magwitch and Compeyson are committed to the Hulks at the end of chapter 5 their particular Hulk is described as looking 'like a wicked Noah's ark'. They have entered it to be imprisoned; the animals and humans entered the ark in Genesis 7 'two and two' to be saved. Pip's quest for his parents has, in other words, made him obsessed with couples. It is little surprise, then, that the lost parents of chapter 1, who turn out in one way to 'be' Adam and Eve, should be shadowed by another pair: quarrelling and aggressive Magwitch and Compeyson (and notice how Compeyson's presence is anticipated in the figure of the imaginary young man invented by Magwitch to terrify Pip into compliance in chapter 1. When Pip sees Compeyson in chapter 3 he thinks he is the young man). Magwitch and Compeyson are one of the novel's manifestations of Abel and Cain, whose story is told in Genesis 4. Abel and Cain are, then, in Pip's febrile imagination, incarcerated in a prison of an ark. What, as they say, on earth is going on?

Let's go back to the ark for a moment. Genesis 6 tells us that the destruction of the earth took place because it 'was corrupt before God ... all flesh had corrupted his way upon the earth'. Humanity has corrupted God's ways; and flesh itself is, because of the Fall, corrupt. Dickens seems to elaborate this point with characteristic symbolic resonance in chapter 20, where a Jew excitedly approaches Jaggers with the chant, '"Oh Jaggerth, Jaggerth, Jaggerth! all otherth ith Cag-Maggerth ..."'. *Maggers* is meant to recall *Mag*-witch, of course; and *cag-mag* is a contemporary slang word for a carcass. More precisely, it denotes meat that, already dead, is passed off by a butcher as having been freshly slaughtered. In chapter 20 it has a horrible resonance in connection with Smithfield. But it also reaches back to the beginning of stage 1 to amplify the already complex implications of Magwitch on the marshes. For this convict who invokes the concept of the transmigration of souls into different forms of flesh in order that he might the better survive on the marshes ('I wish I was a frog. Or a eel!') is, as a piece of cag-mag, corrupt flesh in all its postlapsarian lostness. The Darwinian sense that we evolved from the primordial slime glimmers here as a possibility that fades into a conviction that we are doomed by a God who, from the beginning, saw us as exiles, outcasts from His grace compelled to perish in swamp and mire.

But Dickens, for all his doubts (the kind of doubts that rise to the surface of the creatively imaginative mind rather than expressing themselves in more formal discourse), knows that Magwitch is not frog, eel, or anything other than a human being. In this he follows St Paul on resurrection in 1 Corinthians 15:

> All flesh is not the same flesh: but there is one kind of flesh of men, another flesh of beasts ... Behold, I shew you a mystery: We shall not all sleep, but we shall all be changed, In a moment, in the twinkling of an eye, at the last trump... For this corruptible must put on incorruption, and this mortal must put on immortality.

In order to understand resurrection, St Paul has to go back to Adam, made of earth, and rework in his mind the relationship between earth and heaven, matter and spirit. In a similar way Dickens, having created in Magwitch an image of the archetypal bemired outcast, both Adam and a survivor of the flood, rethinks him. If he is a man of sorrows and thus Christlike, he is also, as we are told much later, 'Magwitch ... chrisen'd Abel' (chapter 40): cag-mag *and* God's favourite son from Genesis 4. And so, when Pip sees Magwitch's double (Compeyson) in chapter 3 and then, with Joe and the soldiers, comes across the two fighting and the word *murder* is dropped into the text, we know that Compeyson is Cain.

The story of Abel and Cain is located in Genesis between those of the Fall and the Flood. In *Great Expectations* it appears at the beginning after we sense that Pip is seeking for his lost Adam and Eve and before the pair of convicts is relegated to the ark of a Hulk. It was a favourite with Dickens and, as in *Our Mutual Friend* (1864–5), the novel that succeeded *Great Expectations*, is associated in his mind with the concept of the *double* (the twinned pair in that novel, Bradley Headstone and Rogue Riderhood, who are equivalent in many ways to Magwitch and Compeyson, confront each other in chapter 57 which is entitled 'Better to be Abel than Cain').

The double, a particular commonplace of nineteenth-century literature, is the imagining of another self, either good or bad, to shadow one's real self. An example which had an influence on *Great Expectations* is Mary Shelley's *Frankenstein* (1818), where the monster is a double for Frankenstein himself. A later instance is Stevenson's *Dr Jekyll and Mr Hyde* (1886). Karl Miller, the latest historian of the concept, notes that the double is usually opposite to one's 'normal' self, that it is one's surrogate as tempter, aggressor, tyrant, and so on (*Doubles: Studies in Literary History*; Oxford: O.U.P., 1985), hitting out where one dare not hit out oneself. Equally, the double may attack or threaten not the imaginer's enemies but the imaginer him- or herself, whom we thus see to be 'engaged in the impossible task of trying to escape from himself' (ibid., p. 47).

This raises all sorts of possibilities for the interpretation of *Great Expectations*, but it suggests primarily how swiftly Pip moves from focusing on the parental pair to concentrating on the father in the form of Magwitch and the father's double, Compeyson. This double who hates Magwitch is Magwitch's other self, the darkly criminal part from which his better self is trying to escape. More profoundly, Compeyson represents Pip as Oedipal hater of his father imagined in the form of Magwitch and perceived as the rival for the affections of his mother. (Note how Compeyson and Magwitch are both linked, as Pip is, to Miss Havisham: Compeyson as her betrayer and Magwitch as the father of her daughter.) If Compeyson hates Magwitch then so, for a long time, does Pip; and a further connection between Compeyson and Pip is that Pip creates and holds Miss Havisham in the prison of his mind, imagining her into existence in Satis, while Compeyson is the one who, in terms of the story, causes her imprisonment. In other words, Compeyson is the agent – acting against Magwitch and Miss Havisham – of Pip's own deepest desires against the father and of his need to conserve the mother in the deathly gaol of bridal virginity.

Compeyson as Cain and Pip's own double harks strangely and significantly back, too, to a moment in Dickens's autobiographical fragment (see Autobiography, above). After his mother has gone to join John Dickens in the Marshalsea, the young Charles, still at the blacking warehouse, had to go into lodgings and there, outcast from his family by location and occupation, saw himself as Cain: 'and I (small Cain that I was, except that I had never done harm to any one) was handed over as a lodger to a reduced old lady . . .'

Dickens here, like Pip, conforms brilliantly to Miller's perception that double fantasies occur more frequently in connection with the idea (or actuality) of orphanhood than in any other situation. Cut off from one's parents, either in real life or in imagination because one feels 'other' than them, one imagines into existence another self to punish them, taunt them, or whatever.

The characteristic posture of Magwitch and Compeyson throughout the novel is one of struggle and opposition, with Compeyson mirroring a very real element of Pip's feelings for Magwitch. When the word *murder* is mentioned in chapter 5 we are plunged straight into the fallen world of Genesis 4: Adam and Eve beget Cain and then Abel, 'a keeper of sheep'. Jealous because God appears to prefer Abel's offerings to his own, 'Cain rose up against Abel his brother, and slew him' and is punished by the threat of wandering over the surface of the earth and dwelling 'on the east of Eden'.

Murder is thus the direct first result of original sin. The Genesis landscape of the opening of *Great Expectations* drops the idea of original sin before us, combines the problem of murder with that of survival in a Darwinian world (hence the sergeant's 'confound you for two wild beasts' as he tries to separate the two struggling men in chapter 5) and then starts to unravel a world of incredible psychological complexity as it invites us to recognize and question the origin of this kind of impulse, through Pip's experience, in ourselves. The Pip whose narrating voice we hear and are entertained by is, we gradually realize with horror, not just the Compeyson-(and Cain-)like hater of Magwitch in any minimal or purely formal sense: that is, the notion isn't released into the novel at the beginning merely to be dropped. It reappears with Magwitch and becomes the main focus of the novel. For when Magwitch returns in chapter 39 and tells Pip that he made his money as a sheep farmer, and Pip records in obsessive physical detail his loathing of the man, we realize forcibly how Cain-like Pip is in relation to this Abel. And since this is the chapter in which Magwitch calls himself Pip's

27

'second father', we are compelled to acknowledge too how inseparably connected parricide and Cain-like fratricide are in Pip's mind. The attempt to bury Magwitch has not worked (or rather, it has worked only on the level of the rational mind: he was relegated to the Hulk and apparently forgotten). Pip's unconscious mind breaks through again, as it did at the beginning of the novel. Magwitch returns, dominating Pip's life.

Even before that, of course, Magwitch has been a felt presence, registering himself through shadows and images and thus not so much obliterated by being forgotten as threateningly imminent. Hence the stranger at the inn in chapter 10 who returns himself in chapter 28. Yet even he emphasizes the Cain–Abel relationship between Pip and Magwitch as much as he does anything else. On his reappearance he mutters on about the two one-pound notes, which have obvious symbolic affinity with the two plaster casts in Jaggers's office and with the Cain–Abel theme as it starts with the two struggling convicts. When we first see him, though, he produces the file that links Pip with Magwitch in conspiracy and in loathing and that also develops into a symbolic finger pointing out Pip's guilt to him (Jaggers's in chapter 11, the village finger-post in chapter 19 which has been an image of guilt as early on as chapter 3). Clearly, the fingers do not point merely at guilt as such but specifically at the guilt that is located in the impulse to murder as portrayed in the primal murder of sibling by sibling in Genesis 4.

Indeed, once we are attuned to the presence of Cain and Abel as determinants in Pip's narrative (and thus his psychic life), we notice how omnipresent they are. Everyone in pursuit of the two convicts in chapter 5 'slanted to the right (where the East was)'; Pip is exiled to the East at the end (conclusion of chapter 58, opening of chapter 59); Magwitch's return in between is announced by a persistent east wind (opening of chapter 39). Much of the novel's action, in fact, occurs 'east of Eden'.

Moreover, Pip's Cain-like behaviour towards Magwitch is duplicated in his behaviour to Joe: equal rather than father and hence, in effect, brother (chapter 2), Pip soon disowns him. And notice how crucial Joe is to the theme. For he is a pacifist, for reasons that he explains in chapter 7 after Magwitch has been committed to oblivion. Joe's father was a drunkard and a wife-beater. He died and then Joe's mother died and Joe profited by his example: 'I'm dead afeerd of going wrong in the way of not doing what's right by a woman'. Although ready to challenge those who affront him (Orlick in chapter 15, Jaggers in chapter 18, etc.), Joe is essentially a muscular non-combatant who has rejected the Cain-like violence he was brought up on, asserting his constant willingness to be his brother's keeper (as in his treatment of the infant Pip, of Magwitch, and so forth). In addition, he has found a way of undoing the Oedipal conflict that so bedevils Pip. By an act of *imagination* and *sympathy* (but not identification), Joe imagines the tyrant father into a being of goodness, if not of action then at least of intention. The testament to this is the epitaph Joe composed for him and of which he is so proud, and which he meant to have had engraved for his father's tombstone: 'Whatsume'er the failings on his part, Remember reader he were that good in his hart' (chapter 7).

Now that should, of course, be the message Pip takes away from his own father's tombstone. The fact that it isn't engenders Magwitch, Compeyson, Abel, Cain – indeed, the whole problematic narrative that is *Great Expectations*. Above all it marks Pip as Cain almost everywhere, even at Satis. He may keep himself under control on his first visit, but on his second visit (chapter 11) he fights 'the pale young gentleman' Herbert Pocket as Magwitch fought Compeyson. And notice Pip's guilt feelings afterwards and the way he identifies himself 'as a species of savage young wolf, or other wild beast'. The guilt spills over, like Herbert's blood, into the opening of chapter 12 where Pip, discovering 'traces of [Herbert's] gore ... covered them with garden-mould from the eye of man' in a gesture which seems to be based on his fear that he has re-enacted Genesis 4:11 ('now art thou cursed from the earth, which had opened her mouth to receive thy brother's blood from thy hand').

In this connection it should be noted that when Pip and Herbert meet up again – as in this novel of repetition and return they inevitably do – at the beginning of stage 2 (chapter 21), they establish a friendship that is based on Herbert's failure as a suitor to Estella (chapter 22). Had he still been a suitor Pip's Cain-like jealousy would have continued. Now that he is no longer a rival, he and Pip can be 'harmonious', the Herbert-Abel coexisting with his subdued Cain of a friend. At this point, too, Herbert can be presented, like Joe in stage 1, as a moral positive and Pip's good double:

Herbert Pocket had a frank and easy way with him that was very taking. I had never seen any one then and I have never seen any one since, who more strongly expressed to me, in every look and tone, a natural incapacity to do anything secret and mean. (chapter 22)

29

Herbert, with his lack of secretiveness, like Joe and his gentle woman's touch (chapter 13), is the exact opposite of Pip as an imaginer of a dark world inhabited by Magwitch, Compeyson, Jaggers, Orlick and Miss Havisham; the fantasist of a vampire-like Estella (the sign of which is the 'bright flush upon her face' at the end of chapter 11), the imprisoner of Miss Havisham in a black hearse of a coach (chapter 9), the man who insists on the depths of the 'secrecy there is in the young, under terror' (end of chapter 2).

We do not get too far into stage 1, however, without being introduced explicitly, rather than implicitly, to a Cain in the person of Orlick, someone else who is intimately connected with the marshes:

He was a broad-shouldered loose-limbed swarthy fellow of great strength, never in a hurry, and always slouching. He never even seemed to come to his work on purpose, but would slouch in as if by mere accident; and when he went to the Jolly Bargemen to eat his dinner, or went away at night, he would slouch out, like Cain or the Wandering Jew, as if he had no idea where he was going and no intention of ever coming back. He lodged at a sluice-keeper's out on the marshes . . . (chapter 15)

Orlick batters Mrs Joe into submission (same chapter), shadows Pip when he is out with Biddy, the astute girl whom he thinks he loves with his rational, daylight *persona* or self and who is thus the good double of Estella (chapter 17), and struggles with Pip in the old sluice-house on the marshes (as Magwitch struggles with Compeyson), calling him *wolf* and telling him 'it was you as did for your shrew sister' (chapter 53).

If Compeyson functions as Pip's double with respect to Magwitch (his name, as E. L. Gilbert has pointed out, obviously derives from *compaysan*: that is, co-patriot; one who lives with you as a son of the same fatherland), then Orlick is Pip's double as woman-hater, that darkest of all aspects of the Oedipal mentality.

The logic of Pip's thinking in this respect seems to run as follows (I am imagining the 'thoughts' of his unconscious as I infer them from the narrative he gives us): yearning for dead mother and awareness of dead father leads to visit to parental graves which leads in turn to the symbolic opening up of the graves as Magwitch leaps up and Satis reveals the dead mother as Miss Havisham/Chavah (universal mother, Eve), who as a bride is the image of his sexual desire but who is also forbidding and hence forbidden because horrifying and old. At which point, enter Estella as sexually attractive young version of the mother who is nevertheless still prohibited (by being of a higher social caste) and prohibiting (she is rude to him and draws attention to his inferiority). (We should reflect, however, that it is Estella whom Pip meets first as a result of the Miss Havisham-mother's invitation to go to Satis. Estella thus directs him to the reality of his vision, as if his unconscious is saying through her: your mother is not the object of your (however unattainable) sexual adoration after all: look at her; she is old and terrible.) Meanwhile, back at the forge, Mrs Joe pummels and batters him, berating him for ever having been born (chapter 2), a mother who is no mother. Or rather, a mother who conforms to what Freud, with that obtuseness that characterizes his attempts to understand the nature of the feminine, termed the 'phallic mother', a woman who is aggressively, punitively and fear-inducingly male in her behaviour (see, for example, his *New Introductory Lectures on Psycho-analysis*, lectures 29 and 33; *Standard Edition*, vol. 22, pp. 24 and 126–30).

It is this figure, then, so dominant in Pip's earlier childhood, whom Pip's Orlick self kills off. And she is killed, presumably, so that the 'fairy godmother' Miss Havisham (chapter 19), together with her attendant Estella, may hold full sway over Pip's narrative and, the same thing, his fantasies. Except that Mrs Joe is not actually killed straight away. With an appalling touch of sadism Pip keeps her lingering, committing her to a long period of vegetative incapacity, her punishment for having been unkind to him in infancy. The battering of her with the leg-iron by Orlick parallels the hammering given to Joe's mother by the drunken father (chapter 7). Orlick's action as Pip's double tells us, in fact, that Pip is quite clearly someone who should never marry because he has the mind of a wife-batterer. This aspect of Pip and Orlick finds its culmination in the figure of Bentley Drummle, who marries then maltreats Estella in chapter 59.

3. Inset: *George Barnwell* and Pip the Apprentice
chapter 15

It is a particular feature of *Great Expectations* that, like an eighteenth-century novel or Renaissance play or poem, it focuses crucial areas of its meaning through an inset text (see Pip's Journey by Instalments and by Stages, above). In *Hamlet* that text is the play-within-the-play called *The Mousetrap*, that 'image of a murder done in Vienna' which discloses Claudius's brother-killing Cain-like self to us by re-enacting the murder that is prior to, and the impetus behind, the play of *Hamlet* itself. Since *The Mousetrap* enshrines *Hamlet*'s deepest secret it is presented at the literal centre – the heart – of the play. At the centre of *Great Expectations*, give or take a chapter or two, we find the most significant of the three inset texts, *Hamlet* (chapter 31). In stage 1 the *Hamlet* theme of murder is anticipated through the insertion of a reading of George Lillo's *The London Merchant; or, the History of George Barnwell*, a sentimental tragedy. Wopsle, Pip's actor double, performs it before him in Pumblechook's parlour towards the end of chapter 15, the chapter which begins with Pip, now Joe's apprentice, still yearning for Estella, introduces us to Orlick, and concludes with the attack on Mrs Joe.

The play's plot is as follows: George Barnwell is an apprentice who is seduced into loving a prostitute, Sarah Millwood. She persuades him to rob his master and to rob and murder his uncle. When all the money is spent she informs on him and they are both imprisoned and hanged.

Barnwell's London setting and its linking of greed and murder make rather ominous the comic song Pip has just learned from Biddy ('When I went to Lunnon town sirs . . .') and puts a hangman's noose of a question mark over his status as a good apprentice. This is how Pip describes his experience of *Barnwell*:

No sooner did [Wopsle] see me, than he appeared to consider that a special Providence had put a 'prentice in his way to be read at . . . when Mr Wopsle got into Newgate, I thought he never would go to the scaffold, he became so much slower than at any former period of his disgraceful career. I thought it a little too much that he should complain of being cut short in his flower after all, as if he had not been running to seed, leaf after leaf, ever since his course began . . . What stung me, was the identification of the whole affair with my unoffending self . . . I was made to murder my uncle with no extenuating circumstances whatever; Millwood put me down in argument, on every occasion . . . Even after I was happily hanged and Wopsle had closed the book, Pumblechook sat staring at me, and shaking his head, and saying, 'Take warning, boy, take warning!' as if it were a well-known fact that I contemplated murdering a near relation, provided I could only induce one to have the weakness to become my benefactor.

Note how Pip, from being unwilling spectator and assistant, is drawn into Wopsle's own part of the vicious and murdering Barnwell, so that the attack on Mrs Joe within a page or so implicates Pip and couples him with the real attacker, Orlick the journeyman, whom Pip and Wopsle discover on their way home slouching around 'on the chance of company' rather as Pip was loitering in the High Street when Wopsle picked him up. (The companion to this chapter is, in many ways, chapter 53, the last encounter with Orlick in the sluice-house when the attack on Mrs Joe is relived shortly after 9 p.m., the novel's symbolic hour. The *Barnwell*-reading finishes at 'half-past nine o'clock'.)

And yet it is, after all, Wopsle who acts Barnwell (as it will be Wopsle who takes the part of Hamlet) and Pumblechook who accuses Pip. Both may try to turn him into Barnwell but he is, actually, a character in his own novel, not an inhabitant of Lillo's play, as Dickens reminds us by making Wopsle 'close the book' in a self-referentially literary action designed to demonstrate exactly this fact: that Pip inhabits a different world (or book) and that his history is not necessarily Barnwell's. Pumblechook's insistence that Pip *is* somehow Barnwell (and Pip's apparent agreement) raises all sorts of questions: about Pip's awareness of his own guilt and the question of freedom of action (can he break free of the Barnwell parallel, or is it one more instance of the repetition and determinism that I have already drawn attention to in the novel?); about the extent to which the characters who people Pip's narrative are images of his guilt; and so on.

Nevertheless it would appear that from the point of view of Pip's inmost self it makes little difference if Wopsle has closed the book or not since it is that self that seized on *Barnwell* in the first place, pulling guilt out of the air whenever it can. Pip reads *Barnwell* as he reads the tombstones, with the eye of his imagination, and he invites us to do the same by dropping so many clues to the parallels between his life and the play that it would be an act of readerly churlishness to ignore them.

The immediate roots of Pip's identification with Barnwell lie in chapter 13 when he is formally bound apprentice with all the resentment against Joe and against home that this finally brings to the forefront of his mind. Yet Pip's resentment at being committed to Joe has less to do with being branded worker rather than gentleman, I suspect, than it has with his sense that being bound apprentice, as a formal contract, re-enacts his mother's abandoning of him to Joe and Mrs Joe by her death. In other words, he sees the handing over of himself together with the 25 guineas as child-selling: his symbolic mother is contractually registering her separation from him (and thus ritualizing his separation anxiety) and setting the seal upon it with money. Being *bound* apprentice mocks the umbilical link he retains psychologically with his mother(s) – represented in this instance by Miss Havisham – and confirms his link as a growing male with the world of the fathers by reminding us of Magwitch's chains, the chains on the Hulks, and Jaggers's watch chain (chapter 25). More than that, *binding* does not just remind *us* of Magwitch, it reminds Pip of him too, reiterating in yet another way his identification with the shameful humiliation, bestiality and poverty of the convict world. Work at the forge will enable Pip to shoe a horse but not own one; to undo the links on fetters but not to escape from fetters. It imprisons Pip, who will not see that Estella and Miss Havisham are both imprisoned, and that prisons are not always of the law's or authority's making but can be the product of one's own willed fantasies.

Pip's reluctance to be bound elicits a reaction from the outside world, which picks up his sense of his own guilt. Feeling like a malefactor, a condemned Barnwell who has already killed his relative on behalf of a woman who is, he thinks, socially far above him, he becomes a malefactor. The crowd condemn him and he is taken before the Justices to be bound (which echoes the trial of Barnwell and anticipates Magwitch's own trial at the end) but not before a 'person of mild and benevolent aspect ... gave me a tract ornamented with a woodcut of a malevolent young man fitted up with a perfect sausage-shop of fetters, and entitled, TO BE READ IN MY CELL'.

Image now repeats image as Pip, anticipating himself as Barnwell in the condemned cell, here sees himself as the malefactor framed by linked sausages of fetters which, via Wemmick's pig (which will be made into sausages in chapter 45) and Pumblechook's gluttonous apostrophes to pork and to Pip as the young Squeaker (chapter 4), hark back to Magwitch as Legion (p. 18 above), his devils now running riot in these particular pork sausages. (Not that the text of chapter 13 actually names them as pork; but, given the imagistic structure of the novel as a whole, they could scarcely be anything else.) Pip is making his imaginary history – his identification with the convict father – come true. As an apprentice he is more bound than he was as a child. The irony is that when he breaks free to be a gentleman he will be bound even closer to Magwitch.

Pip thus returns home 'with the strong *conviction* on me that I should never like Joe's trade' (end of chapter 13). Repudiating the Joe father (despite recognizing his good qualities) makes Pip a Prodigal Son (the son in Luke 15 also has rather a lot to do with swine, as Wopsle recalls in chapter 4) as well as someone harbouring Cain-like feelings, the nature and degree of which are underlined for us if we recall the murder scene in *Barnwell* where, after murdering his uncle, Barnwell exclaims:

> Murder the worst of crimes, and parricide the worst of murders, and this the worst of parricides. Cain, who stands on record from the birth of time and must to its final period as accursed, slew a brother favoured above him ... But I ... have murdered a brother, mother, father, and a friend most loving and beloved. (Regents Restoration Drama Series edn, ed. W. H. McBurney (1965), III, vii)

Pip, of course, thinks he has murdered his own 'uncle', Pumblechook, in chapter 4.

Pip's comment on Wopsle's Barnwell – 'I thought it a little too much that he should complain of being cut short in his flower after all, as if he had not been running to seed, leaf after leaf, ever since his course began ...' – implicates Pip in Barnwell's conspiracy against the uncle, too: Pip is, after all, a pip which is only too eager to flower and run to seed, and it is probably no accident that he has started to think in terms of seeds and flowers on his first entry into his uncle's shop in chapter 8, when he has also seen it as a prison:

> I wondered when I peeped into one or two [drawers] on the lower tiers, and saw the tied-up brown paper packets inside, whether the flower-seeds and bulbs ever wanted of a fine day to break out of those jails, and bloom.

This makes Pumblechook the gaoler of 'pip', to put it simply. What it suggests is that Pip can only become more than a pip by overthrowing the Pumblechook father. Barnwell's seeds and flowers invite us to see in Pip's struggle with his adult male relatives a reminder of the analogy between the seasonal cycle and the necessary supersession of the older generation by the younger. Fathers have to die – or be killed. Zany fulfilment of Pip's fantasies in this respect comes in that wonderful moment in chapter 57 when Joe reports how Orlick robbed Pumblechook, stuffed his mouth with flowering annuals, and is temporarily in the county gaol. Which is as much as to say that Pip's exuberant Cain of a double gets away (almost) with murder in order to exist on the margins of civilization as a perpetual challenge to authority.

What Pip actually regards himself as accused of as he sits in Pumblechook's parlour is murder of a 'near relation, provided I could only induce one to have the weakness to become my benefactor'. This, of course, includes Magwitch as one of Pip's intended victims while at the same time teasing us with the certainty of murderous thoughts towards Miss Havisham, a certainty confirmed by the circumstances of Miss Havisham's death. For it is long and lingering, though not as long as Mrs Joe's; and she is laid when dead on a table just as Mrs Joe is seen by Pip 'lying without sense or movement on the bare boards where she had been knocked down . . .'. It is as if hearing from Miss Havisham about her deathbed scenario in chapter 11 has not only supplied him with the details of Mrs Joe's attack here but has also induced him, through his agent Orlick, to carry it out.

4. More Biblical Textures

(a) ADAMIC LABOUR AND GENTILITY

We saw earlier that Dickens creates postlapsarian wildernesses out of the churchyard and Satis's rank garden, peopling them with a primal parental pair in the form of Magwitch (an earthy Adam emerging from and disappearing into the mud of the marsh country) and Miss Havisham (a remote and fossilized Eve); that in coupling Magwitch with Compeyson he produces an Abel and Cain pair; and that the description of the prison ship as 'a wicked Noah's ark' is no merely incidental rhetorical flourish since the pairs which people the novel can be seen as having emerged from it into a mocking parody of the new post-Flood creation of Genesis 8. The Hulks float on mud and ooze; and every time a convict appears to Pip (like the stranger in chapter 10 who reappears in chapter 28) we get the sense that the criminal old Adam in Pip is pressing very close indeed to the threshold of his consciousness, especially since this particular convict conjures back into Pip's fancy 'the wicked Noah's Ark lying out on the black water' (end of chapter 28). And in the sense that the lower reaches of the Thames towards Gravesend remind Pip explicitly of the Kent marsh country of his childhood (chapter 54) to which he returns in the final chapter, the mud which is so quintessentially Adamic (because of the meaning of the name Adam) dominates the novel's physical structure, too. Meanwhile, the convict's definition of Pip's homeland as 'mudbank, mist, swamp, and work; work, swamp, mist, and mudbank' (chapter 28) emphasizes the connection between marsh and postlapsarian Adamic labour, God's sentencing of Adam in Genesis 3:19 to work 'in the sweat of thy face'.

Following this line of thought, Pip's self-consciousness about his coarseness and commonness, and his commitment to the graves of his parents – that earth in which they are buried – can be seen as over-awareness of his role as a son of Adam, awareness reinforced by the name of his mother, Georgiana (see p. 21 above). Pip's determination to become a gentleman is therefore an attempt to eradicate his Adamic self through the power of Mammon, so that he undergoes material re-formation rather than spiritual reformation.

Magwitch makes this clear in chapter 39 when he says to Pip: 'I worked hard that you should be above work.'

Our clue to the gentility theme from this point of view is the proverb, 'When Adam delved and Eve span/Who was then the gentleman?', which asserts a vision of human community and equality very similar to that which lies at the heart of *Great Expectations* and which is resolved thematically when Pip recognizes base Joe as 'this gentle Christian man' (chapter 57). The theme has already been anticipated by Matthew Pocket, however, with his belief that 'no man who was not a true gentleman at heart, ever was, since the world began, a true gentleman in manner' (chapter 22). Note how the phrase *since the world began* is, once more, a thematic rather than merely incidental detail, since it takes us back to Adam in the Genesis creation myth again. Matthew continues: 'the more varnish you put on, the more the grain will express itself', which is significant because the alternative to identifying gentility with externals (varnish) is the laying aside of worldly goods and the discovery of truth in unlikely places, which includes the perception that Magwitch, for all his convict's garb, is a figure of magical power. This is something his name suggests, as does his identification with the hanged pirate at the end of chapter 1. For the hanged man is a symbol of the father as god, mysteriously suspended between, and thus linking, earth and sky (J. E. Cirlot, *A Dictionary of Symbols*, tr. Jack Sage (London: Routledge and Kegan Paul, 1962), pp. 131–2). This notion in turn relates to that literalistic puzzle Pip has over the gravestone inscription in chapter 7: 'I read "wife of the Above" as a complimentary reference to my father's exaltation to a better world'. And this in turn implies that Pip's quest for gentility has its origins in an equivalent literalism when we read that Miss Havisham and Estella are 'far above the level of such common doings' as sitting in the kitchen (chapter 9). And note how the idea of the elevated father is reworked in connection with Bill Barley, the father of Herbert's fiancée Clara: invisible to all except Clara he is perpetually up above, experienced only through the curses, growls, and knocking that are heard through the beams of the ceiling (chapter 46).

(b) PENITENCE AND PENITENTIARIES

Miss Havisham has a broken heart that she has transmitted to Estella in the form of a heartlessness that is the opposite of the concept of the good heart as expressed in Joe's epitaph for his father (chapter 7). On one level a statement about the importance of memory and reputation in bestowing immortality upon the dead, on another the epitaph repeats Matthew Pocket's definition of gentility as a matter of heart. Matthew's concept itself, however, has its roots in the New Testament's association of spirituality with soundness of heart and rejection of the Christian message with hardness of heart (Mark 3, 6; John 12; Acts 19, etc.). More specifically still, a hard heart is associated with *impenitence* (Romans 2:5: 'thy hardness and impenitent heart') and so releases another major linguistic and spiritual concern in *Great Expectations*: that of penitence.

Heart and penitence are linked in chapter 30 when Pip's commitment to Estella makes him fail to visit Joe: 'I arrived in London safe – but not sound, for my heart was gone. As soon as I arrived, I sent a penitential codfish and barrel of oysters to Joe'. His heart is now Estella's, the passage reminds us. It is also 'gone' (hardened) with respect to Joe, who has to receive fishy manifestations of guilt that should more appropriately be eaten by a penitent Pip. What, then, is the place of penitence in the novel?

We first encounter the concept when Joe emerges to go to church on Christmas Day in his 'full suit of Sunday penitentials' (chapter 4). It reappears in chapter 8 when Pip recalls Mrs Joe's treatment of him as a child ('through all my punishments, disgraces, fasts and vigils, and other penitential performances'); in chapter 9 (Pip 'was overtaken by penitence' at telling lies to Joe about Miss Havisham; a page later he 'sit[s] down in the ashes at [Joe's] feet'); in chapter 12 (where Pip feels little penitence at the prospect of hurting Pumblechook), and chapter 13: Joe, in his Sunday clothes again, is off to see Miss Havisham about Pip's indentures while Mrs Joe leads the way carrying various items either 'penitentially or ostentatiously'. Although the word *repentance* occurs later, as at the beginning of chapter 28 ('in the first flow of my repentance it was equally clear that I must stay at Joe's'), *penitence* and its derivatives occur most frequently in stage 1.

Its function is to place Pip's guilt – for having been born, for having imagined Magwitch into existence, etc. – in a Christian context of reformation. Penitence is a ritual acknowledgement of, and way of purging, one's sins. Typically it requires self-mortification, or submission of the self to some other penalty. As far as the novel goes, though, the problem is that whereas the church has a long list of sins which it is easy enough to recognize and try to repent of, Pip finds himself in a world which accuses him – in the form of Mrs Joe, Pumblechook, the village finger-post, Jaggers's finger, and so on – of guilt and sin for which Dickens, as Pip's creator, in the end refuses to supply theological justification. Like the images of fallenness in the novel, the word *penitence* evokes a Christian concept only to query and then to deny its validity.

This means that all that is left of the notion of penitence is accusation and punishment, and that these are applied not in order to effect reformation of the inner self but simply to wound and hurt. The implications of this for the novel emerge clearly from chapter 4 where, after mentioning Joe's Sunday penitentials, Pip is led to comment on his own childhood clothes:

As to me, I think my sister must have had some general idea that I was a young offender whom an Accoucheur Policeman had taken up (on my birthday) and delivered over to her, to be dealt with according to the outraged majesty of the law. I was always treated as if I had insisted on being born, in opposition to the dictates of reason, religion, and morality, and against the dissuading arguments of my best friends. Even when I was taken to have a new suit of clothes, the tailor had orders to make them like a kind of Reformatory, and on no account to let me have the free use of my limbs.

Clothes, in other words, become a prison or penitentiary: the idea of spiritual reformation is lost to the grotesque notion of the punitive re-formation of Pip's vulnerable infant limbs through the force of stiff, ill-cut, cloth. Thus Pip, on his birthday, was, in Mrs Joe's eyes, accompanied into the world by a policeman for a midwife and labelled 'convict'. The parallel with his later experience of being bound apprentice in chapter 15 is obvious, and again betrays the connection there is in Pip's mind between all his mother figures: this time the Miss Havisham who hands him over to be bound is seen not just to parallel the real mother who has let him down by dying but also Mrs Joe, the sister-mother who hedged his infancy round with images of arresting and hand-cuffing policemen (there is, of course, a pun in *cuff* which recalls the punitive aspect of being brought up 'by hand'). Note also, though, the way the binding of Pip in his clothes anticipates his later problems as a gentleman, his lack of ease as he inhabits the external signs of a gentility he is aware of not possessing inwardly.

As this passage primarily reminds us, though, the middle of the nineteenth century was a period particularly concerned with prisons and criminality. Chaplains were still seen (as indeed they are today) as an essential ingredient in prison-staffing and the staffing of reformatories and penitentiaries, but their role was in practice marginal because, as I have said, prisoners' physical punishments and deprivations were understood increasingly as ends in themselves rather than as aids to spiritual and moral reformation. They were not, in other words, signals of repentance.

Penitentiary houses had first been established in the 1770s, some ninety years before *Great Expectations* was written, as reformatories for the more hardened criminals: 'The term Penitentiary clearly shows that Parliament had chiefly in view the reformation and amendment of those to be committed to such places of confinement'; and the amendment was to be achieved by placing offenders in 'solitary imprisonment, accompanied by well-regulated labour, and religious instruction' (John Howard, *An Account of Lazarettos* (1789); in his *The State of the Prisons*, Everyman edn (London and New York, 1929), pp. 260–61). In the nineteenth century, however, things were rather different, and this moved Dickens to see the whole problem more fundamentally, with the eye of the social realist rather than that of the visionary reformer. In this novel he asks the question: what is the point of a prison system if, as the juxtaposition of Pip's infant history with his reformatory clothes and Magwitch's history as recounted in chapter 42 implies, many of us – perhaps most of us – are 'just born' into deprivation, accusation and guilt? The prison system works hand in hand with the established church to consolidate our sense of our original sin. But what, this novel asks, quietly yet increasingly insistently, if we reject the concept of original sin as a vile conspiratorial fiction? It is in such instances that Dickens comes closest of all to Marx.

(c) ARKS

If *penitence* shades into *penitentiary* in the novel in a significant rather than merely punning way, then *Hulks* when described as the *ark* have an equally significant part in the thematic structure of *Great Expectations*. The Hulk to which Magwitch is committed was recognized as a particularly punitive form of imprisonment which had little, if any, avowed reformative function (see the *Oxford English Dictionary*, s.v. hulk). As derelict vessels – mere hulls or shells – they were filled with convicts who suffered a high incidence of disease due to overcrowding and lack of nourishment. They therefore become for Dickens images of utter corruption and hopelessness. They are referred to twice in the novel as 'wicked Noah's arks' (chapters 5 and 28). I have already commented on this in connection with the novel's Darwinian theme of evolutionary struggle (section 2 above, 'Cain and Abel'). What I want to concentrate on now is the place of the ark as a symbol of baptismal regeneration, the biblical text for which is I Peter 3: 19–21 ('[Christ] went and preached unto the spirits in prison; Which sometimes were disobedient, when once the longsuffering of God waited in the days of Noah, while the ark was a preparing, wherein few, that is, eight souls were saved by water. The like figure whereunto even baptism doth also now save us ... by the resurrection of Jesus Christ'). Before doing so, however, it is worth recalling how closely the ark and prison hulks were connected in the Victorian mind. Robert Chambers in his *Book of Days: A Miscellany of Popular Antiquities* (1869), for instance, commented that the prisoners who entered the very first hulk on the Thames in July 1776 did so 'chained two and two by the leg', thereby implicitly, if not explicitly, evoking the entry of the creatures 'two and two' in Genesis 7:9. Dickens is thus, as so often, brilliantly developing the symbolic possibilities of an image that is already current.

When Magwitch is dragged back into that 'wicked Noah's ark' at the end of chapter 5 he is disappearing, as if in Charon's boat, into hell. Both he and Compeyson are, as criminals, being relegated to damnation while, Dickens implies, the church stands by and acquiesces in what is happening to them. The Hulk as ark, like penitence, promises remission from sin then withdraws the promise, and in doing so reminds us how far the world of the novel is from that of Christian consolation. Although in many ways a psychological study, *Great Expectations* offers enough of a social vision to suggest the extent of Dickens's anger at the deprivation that the established church, as a privileged middle-class and aristocratic institution, chose, Pharisee-like, to ignore.

It is characteristic of the church as it appears in this novel that it should disappoint Wopsle by refusing to 'throw itself open' (chapter 4) because it is not open to any needy human creature. And it is no surprise either that the Town Hall which is the site of Pip's being bound apprentice should remind him of a church (indeed, it has higher pews than a church) and, with its seated Justices, should anticipate Magwitch's trial at the end (chapter 56) with its thirty-two prisoners 'penned in the dock' to hear their sentences from the Judge as he imitates the judging Christ of Doomsday:

The sun was striking in at the great windows of the court, through the glittering drops of rain upon the glass, and it made a broad shaft of light between the two-and-thirty and the Judge, linking both together, and perhaps reminding some among the audience, how both were passing on, with absolute equality, to the greater Judgment that knoweth all things and cannot err.

After what we have seen and heard of human depravity and deprivation in *Great Expectations*, this sounds rather pietistic and sentimental. Yet it does function thematically as a reminder that one of the novel's messages is equality (Adam as labourer, not gentleman; Compeyson as a public schoolboy of the worst sort; Drummle as a member of the squirearchy who is a brutal Orlick, and so on); that in the eyes of God, despite the fact that the novel so busily questions the goodness and justice of His creation, we are all the same, vulnerable, maimed and pathetic.

The shaft of sunlight makes the point unsubtly, for the sun is a traditional image of the eye of God. In connection with the raindrops, however ('The whole scene starts out again in the vivid colours of the moment, down to the drops of April rain on the windows of the court, glittering in the rays of the April sun'), the sun suggests the imminence, if not the actual presence, of a rainbow, thus returning us once more to Noah's ark, the deluge and the covenant. And we reach this last reminder of the ark symbol through the sophisticated symbolism accompanying Pip's return to his home village in chapter 52. Arrangements having been made for Magwitch's salvation by boat, Pip receives a 'strange letter' demanding his presence at 'the little sluice-house by the limekiln'. So he sets off, putting up not at the main inn, the Blue Boar, but 'at an inn of minor reputation down the town': 'My inn had once been a part of an ancient ecclesiastical house, and I dined in a little octagonal common-room, like a font'.

This in turn recalls the *Hamlet* of chapter 31, where the churchyard scenery for the opening of Act V 'had the appearance of a primeval forest, with a kind of small ecclesiastical wash-house on one side'. The real clue to the meaning of these strange buildings lies in *font* and *wash-house*; for Dickens requires us to recall that fonts are traditionally octagonal in memory of the eight souls who were saved in the ark (see the I Peter 3 quotation at the beginning of this section). So that as a prelude to encountering Orlick, where he will struggle for his life in anticipation of Compeyson's death-struggle with Magwitch, Pip undergoes a symbolic baptism. This baptismal encounter with the font suggests not so much, perhaps, that Pip is having his burden of sin lightened as, rather, that he is, in the true meaning of baptism, finding his spiritual way by dying to his old self (whom he fights in the form of Orlick) in order that he may, eventually, accept Abel Magwitch and be worthy of Joe.

(d) CHRISTMAS AND THE PIGS

The disjunction between Christianity's ideals and the experience of being a human creature in a world that refuses to cushion its inhabitants from its intrinsic harshness by love strikes us forcibly from the second chapter when we discover that Pip encounters Magwitch on Christmas Eve. There is little of the spirit of Christmas in Pip's world – that period of benevolence and fellow feeling which Dickens had identified in the early *Sketches by Boz* (1833–6) when he wrote of 'a magic in the very name of Christmas. Petty jealousies and discords are forgotten' ('Characters', chapter 2). *This* Christmas Eve is notable for the boy's loneliness, Mrs Joe's punitiveness, and Magwitch's desolation: notable, in other words, for the gap between the birth of the Lamb of God who takes away the sins of the world and the criminal and the young boy with their loads on their legs (chapter 2). Pip's Christmas Day begins with his ministrations to Magwitch (chapter 3), partly in the form of food and partly in the form of a file: this is an image of the jubilee promised by Christ's birth (the freeing of slaves and restoration of alienated property to its owners, as in Leviticus 25:10) but rendered also parodic by Mrs Joe's imprecation, which is also an invocation, when Pip returns: '"And where the deuce ha' *you* been?" was Mrs Joe's Christmas salutation, when I and my conscience showed ourselves' (chapter 4; *deuce* is, of course, the devil). All this takes on particular resonance if we remember that *Great Expectations* was serialized from 1 December 1860. For it makes the opening of the novel seasonal in that the serialization coincided with the beginning of Advent, and it suggests as well that Dickens may have been thinking of the novel as an expanded version of one of his Christmas stories, those tales which he produced annually for the Christmas market and which were usually, though not invariably, ghost stories.

The Christmas dinner itself is initiated by Wopsle when he declaims grace in a way that combines the Ghost in *Hamlet* with Richard III (chapter 4), thus reminding us of ghostly Magwitch shivering outside and walking in defiance of that superstition, recorded in *Hamlet*, that ghosts cannot appear at Christmas ('Some say that ever 'gainst that Season comes/Wherein our Saviour's birth is celebrated . . . no spirit dare stir abroad': *Hamlet*, I.i).

But the dinner is perhaps more noteworthy for the discourse on pork that it inspires. The pork of the meal leads Pumblechook to address Pip as a Squeaker and Wopsle to enunciate 'swine were the companions of the prodigal', thereby introducing one of the main biblical texts to underlie *Great Expectations*, that of the prodigal son (see Luke 15), which has more relevance to Pip's history than he cares to admit. Yet his text *does* admit it in a strange symbolic fashion by surrounding Pip with pigs in various forms. The pig of the Christmas feast, together with the pork pie given to Magwitch, both of which confirm Magwitch's affinity with biblical Legion, take on a demonic life of their own, fired by the spirit of Pip's prodigality. Clearly, in *this* narrative the sausage shop that donates the links for the tract in chapter 13 must be a pork butcher. After all, the main inn in Pip's village is the Blue Boar, and when he goes to London he is befriended by a man who keeps a pig at his castle which is, before the novel's end, turned into bacon and sausages (chapter 45).

At this point, though, the porcine theme ceases to be biblical and becomes, rather, a comment on consumerism, the processes by which human societies utilize and process nature's (or maybe evolution's) creatures for their own ends. The swine who are the subject of Wopsle's symbolic exposition develop, even at the hands of kindly Wemmick, into testaments to human exploitation and, as the sausage shop of fetters reminds us, a parable of society's treatment of the criminal and underprivileged: exploiting while claiming to care for them. Further, Pip as Squeaker is recalling his own outrage at Mrs Joe's treatment of him, his awareness, displaced into Pumblechook's mouth, that he too was born only to be the victim of others' needs. Magwitch's exclamation at the beginning – 'what fat cheeks you ha' got . . . Darn Me if I couldn't eat em' – announces the theme, suggesting the link between consumption and consumerism in a predatorily Darwinian way.

The theme – picked up again when Miss Havisham kisses her hand to Estella 'with . . . ravenous intensity' in chapter 29 – takes us back to the Christmas feast. Feeding gluttonously on Christmas Day to celebrate the birth of the Jesus upon whose flesh and blood Wopsle and the rest have been nurtured in communion is, the novel hints, a blasphemy, one which Pip as the bearer of food to the man

45

of sorrows is instinctively aware of. And the theme takes a rather revolting turn at the opening of stage 2 when Pip, waiting for Jaggers's arrival, finds himself in Smithfield: 'the shameful place, being all asmear with filth and fat and blood and foam, seemed to stick to me' (chapter 20). Pip's initial image of London is that it is a meat market which spreads its corruption like a moral taint, as Newgate (which Pip passes in the same paragraph) will later in chapter 32 when Pip visits it with Wemmick while he is waiting for Estella. One of its inmates has a hat with 'a greasy and fatty surface like cold broth'.

As a name, Smithfield links thematically with Pip the blacksmith and with Hammersmith, where the Pocket family lives. But the site of the meat market was also the site of the death of Catholic martyrs under Elizabeth and James I and of Protestant martyrs under Mary Tudor. The Bartholomew Close where Pip finds himself, also in chapter 20, reinforces the association with martyrdom by recalling the St Bartholomew's day massacre of Protestants by Catholics in Paris in 1572. To contemporary London readers all these associations would have combined in their memory of Bartholomew Fair which was held at Smithfield annually for a period which included St Bartholomew's day (August 24) until the middle 1850s. Thus, the religion that began with a baby's birth and a hanging from a cross and has consolidated itself with the blood and flesh of a martyrology has its dark image in the offal of the Smithfield meat market and locates its stain on Jaggers, who insistently washes his hands like Pilate and is known from his first appearance by his scent of soap which, we now understand, masks the taint of meatly corruption he carries with him. When we see him accosted by the two Jews, one of whom chants his 'O Jaggerth, Jaggerth, Jaggerth! all otherth ith Cag-Maggerth . . .', we are therefore not so much in the uneasy territory of Dickens's anti-semitism as at a meeting-point between the Judaeo-Christian world and the brave new world of the mid-Victorian city now being seen, as it is, through the hopeful eyes of the young Pip. If the churchyard of the beginning was an image of an absolutely fallen world unredeemed by Christmas, then Jaggers and the Jews with Smithfield and Bartholomew Close as their backdrop suggest that Pip's next staging-post is no better, that we are all still inhabiting a territory where sin and corruption prevail.

5. Retrospect on Stage 1

The first stage of Pip's expectations is structured around Magwitch, Miss Havisham and the graveyard. The graves of the beginning are recalled by Pip when he revisits the graveyard in chapter 19, though the funeral topography of London will give the lie to Pip's farewell and especially his valediction to Magwitch: 'he was dead to me, and might be veritably dead into the bargain' (chapter 19). This circle – the answering of chapter 1's graveyard by Pip's recollection of it at the opening of the last chapter of stage 1 – has as its centre, in chapter 10, the irruption of the stranger with the file and the two pound notes: in other words, yet another reminder of Magwitch. Either side of this central chapter lies Miss Havisham: Pip's first visit and account of it (chapters 8, 9); and his second visit in chapter 11.

The first half of stage 1 (chapters 1–9) introduces us, therefore, to both Magwitch and Miss Havisham, the Magwitch unit comprising chapters 1–5. From it emerges the problem of the dead parents and of the (apparently) regenerated father who is given a deliberately ghostly quality as he develops an affinity with the hanged pirate who, at the end of chapter 2, explicitly becomes 'a ghostly pirate'. Magwitch involves Pip in guilt against his adoptive parents, Joe and Mrs Joe, as he gets up out of bed at his summons to steal 'wittles'. The complexity of Pip's vision as he realizes the hold this new relationship is beginning to have on him is registered in the way the 'long black horizontal line' of the marshes at the end of chapter 1 becomes the intricate enchaining elaborateness of 'th'meshes' at the end of chapter 2: Pip's linguistic awareness increases in proportion to the degree of his perceptiveness, and puns (fully recognized and enjoyed by children from the age of seven or so) thus become a significant pointer to his increasing realization of the ambivalence of the universe he inhabits. Made to feel guilty by Mrs Joe, he gives birth to Magwitch, who increases his guilt by forcing him to act against Mrs Joe and also Joe by demanding food and a file. The file that will release Magwitch from his chains will enchain Pip in the triple guilt of theft, conspiracy and secrecy (a key notion), turning, as his imagination broods on it, into the file of soldiers with which the Magwitch section ends. The soldiers arrest Magwitch and return him to the Hulks, committing him to a symbolic death and thereby erasing Pip's guilt. In fact, though, this file of soldiers is merely another manifestation of the Accoucheur Policeman who, according to Pip's version of Mrs Joe's reading of family history in chapter 3, attended him into the world and accompanies him in various forms – the pointing finger-post, Jaggers's admonitory forefinger, and so forth – throughout the novel.

The complex of guilt is exacerbated by another pun: criminals are committed to the Hulks for robbing and *forging*, according to Mrs Joe (chapter 2). Pip is already bound, by his promise to Magwitch, to steal; and when he goes in the next chapter to meet him he will stumble across Magwitch's double, Compeyson, who is a forger by trade. But Joe, of course, as village blacksmith, inhabits the forge. *Creating* and *counterfeiting*, in reality recto and verso, obverse and converse, fuse in Pip's mind at this moment as he discovers himself implicated by Magwitch in deceit (doubleness) against forger Joe and his wife. At this point Pip thinks he knows there is a difference between right and wrong but begins to perceive that the moral aspects of the problems posed by the conflicting demands made on him negate such simplicities. In effect he enters a world of moral relativism: stealing for Magwitch is right but induces guilt fostered under the demand for secrecy. Secrecy admits (criminal) complicity. Even though Joe eventually agrees with him Pip is aware that his involvement with Magwitch marks a betrayal of the forge, that he is a hypocrite with respect to Joe and what he represents: that he is, in fact, a faker. As such he forges Compeyson as yet another double for his father, the man who, he thinks, made him what he is. For the real secret, we realize quite early on, is that *Great Expectations* is about Pip's rejection of Joe as father, his quest for someone and something better; and the irony of that secret is that it will turn Pip into a gentleman who is all clothes and little moral and spiritual heart – a fake like Compeyson himself.

Out of the paternal tombstone, then, Pip develops Magwitch-Compeyson as his hybrid father in order to give pedigree and expression to his own 'naterally wicious' nature (chapter 4). The Christmas Day dinner picks up Mrs Joe's sense of outrage at Pip for living and for demanding so much as a child when, as it proceeds, Pip is subjected to the sermon on pork while Joe ladles *gravy* and Pip remembers how Mrs Joe had often wished him in his *grave*. In symbolic revenge for this, Pip 'poisons' another father figure, Pumblechook, later to be so exuberantly awful as Pip's benefactor and patron, but now merely the comic victim of Pip's first attempt at homicide as he plunges and expectorates while Pip clutches at the table leg, regards himself as a Medium communicating with a ghost, and comments, 'I had no doubt I had murdered him somehow' (chapter 4).

Before Miss Havisham is introduced, Pip returns to the churchyard to explain how he reads and misreads the family gravestones (chapter 7). This leads to an account of his education and an example of his writing in the form of an epistle to Joe chalked on his slate, which provokes in turn Joe's autobiographical fragment telling us why he never went to school long enough to learn his letters and about his father's behaviour to his mother.

Joe's autobiographical fragment opens up another window on to the darker places of Pip's own autobiography as it speaks of the function of memory in reverencing one's parents, of redeeming the father and honouring the mother, and reveals how Joe came to be as good as he is. Pip's letter is the dark double of Joe's autobiography, announcing goodwill but containing a destructive subtext that begins to write itself into the plot when Mrs Joe and Pumblechook burst in out of the cold to proclaim that Pip is wanted by Miss Havisham: a mother to replace Mrs Joe and to help Pip erase Joe as well (see Appendix). The degree of rejection that is going on here is registered by an allusion to the murder of Julius Caesar and to Mr Wopsle acting out the part of Revenge from Collins's *Ode on the Passions*. This imagined mother is to elevate him above Joe and the rest of the villagers. Unfortunately, her house is a ship (chapter 8), little different, in its gloomy enchainments, from the Hulks.

The link between Pip's first and second visit to Miss Havisham is, as I have said, the stranger in chapter 10. He is a mystery not just in the sense that he belongs to the suspenseful detective story element in the novel, but in the more fundamental sense that he appears (and remains) unexplained, bearing symbolic tokens. He is secretive, then disappears, leaving Pip and us with the feeling that we have encountered someone from a different order of being. Pip overhears him again in the coach in chapter 28, where he is equally remote and mysterious, a convict who remains unnamed, a passing acquaintance of Magwitch, a voice at once external and internal to Pip's mind.

All we are told of him is that he is 'the stranger', that 'he was a secret-looking man whom I had never seen before', and that he looks 'as if he were taking aim at something with an invisible gun'. He catechizes Pip (as Jaggers will in chapters 11 and 18) and provokes

Wopsle's recitation of Pip's kinship ties with Joe. Then his invisible gun turns into a file and he parts from Pip by giving him a shilling wrapped in 'some crumpled paper' that turns out to be the 'two fat sweltering one-pound notes' that Mrs Joe instantly places in a teapot in the state parlour. The man, who has raised Magwitch's phantom again, haunts Pip's sleep, as does the file.

In his secrecy and strangeness the man is an emblem of the unknown in the novel – that secret within Pip's psyche that the novel itself can express only in the form of symbolic statements about dead parents and graves. He is in a sense an incarnation of Magwitch as unknown father. The two one-pound notes are a floating symbol of the function of money in *Great Expectations*, and in their fat swelteringness and soiled greasiness are a reminder of the fleshy taint that permeates Pip's world, a reminder that Pip and the rest are, like Adam, 'of the earth, earthy' (I Corinthians 15:47), and that there is no such thing as gentility that is not based on the sweat of common clay. (The cruellest reminder of this is remote star-like Estella's parentage in Molly and Magwitch. Another lies in the way the word 'grease' haunts the London section of the novel as a grossly secular and corrupt part-homophone of, and substitute for, the Christian concept of grace.) In their twoness, of course, and, as we discover in chapter 28, their origin with Magwitch, the notes remind us of struggling Magwitch and Compeyson and of the other doubles and couples that dominate the text.

The file – associated with Magwitch because it is the means of his liberation, but also with Joe, whose file it is – becomes, in the stranger's hand, at once bond and pointer. Freudians might wish it to be phallic, but as used in this chapter it is, rather, wand-like, a hieratic staff of office denoting the kind of power and authority embodied in Hermes-Mercury's caduceus which symbolizes his role as intermediary between states of being – the living and dead, heaven and earth – and his power as messenger. For this stranger knows of Pip's connection with Magwitch and so links Pip with that convict of the marshes who is 'dead to' him. Equally, his appearance in the novel seems to be an essential prelude to the second visit to Miss Havisham, whose deathly aura is even more apparent in chapter 11 than it was in chapter 8. He is, then, Pip's guide to the dead and their underworld, a riddling figure who conjoins Magwitch and Miss Havisham in Pip's consciousness. No wonder he induces nightmare disturbances in Pip's sleep.

The gap between the nightmares and Pip's next visit to Miss

Havisham – a full week in contemporary serial readers' time – is in fact minimal. Pip 'scream[s him]self awake' (end of chapter 10) and then, 'at the appointed time' (beginning of chapter 11) rings at the gate and is taken through a long passage in the cellars of the Satis underworld and led across the courtyard into a gloomy low-ceilinged room where the relatives are gathered. The question is, how far is he still in his nightmare? What is the distance, now, between Pip's waking and sleeping self? For it is almost as if the gate is the threshold to a family vault. Pip has, via the stranger this time (as via Pumblechook, the Hades-like imprisoner of seeds last time), entered what is, to all intents and purposes, a burial chamber in which his own lost family is assembled. In it, three ladies and a man listlessly await the pleasure of the 'Witch of the place', dead Miss Havisham, rather like the souls of the dead in Dante's *Inferno*, Virgil's Hades, or T. S. Eliot's *Waste Land*. One of the ladies has the same name as Pip's dead mother (though we are not told this yet) and so, in a way, *is* that much-imagined unfortunate creature. Another, Camilla, 'very much reminded [Pip] of [his] sister' and so, by the same law of dream logic, is an image or shade of that sister, dead as she will be in chapter 35 through the agency of Orlick-Pip. Her face is also described by Pip as a 'dead wall', while another lady speaks 'gravely', thereby initiating a pun that is taken up by Miss Havisham in her airlessly oppressive gravelike room when Pip is conducted to her.

On his way to that room, however, Pip encounters Jaggers, again as yet unnamed, 'groping his way down' through the gloom. Dark and black-bristled with 'a large watch-chain' which, we discover later, is known by the thieves throughout London as something they would steal upon pain of death, he is not so very distinguishable from Magwitch in the gloom of the churchyard encumbered with his chains. The similarity raises once more the novel's fundamental question: gentleman/convict, Cain/Abel, one pound note and another pound note, forger and forger, what is the difference between obverse and converse, who is holding the last link in the chain? Jaggers's similarity to the dark enchained man on the marshes also suggests that Jaggers, too, is an image of the father whom Pip is seeking, caught this time in the act of making his way out of the mother's bedroom. His fat forefinger, which he bites the side of in silent admonishment, parallels the hermetic stranger's file and hints, this time, at a kind of phallic grossness and that he has a suspicion of the Oedipal game that Pip is up to. Otherwise, why should he say: 'Behave yourself . . . boys . . . [are] a bad set of fellows'?

In this chapter, too, Miss Havisham celebrates her birthday by showing Pip the table which she will be laid on when she is dead. In effect, then, Pip has met his dead mother and then been shown her lying-in: her birthday anticipates her funeral feast as, in the first visit, Pip's birth reminded her that she had been living in blackness since he was born. Yet an alternative is introduced into the necrophiliac atmosphere when Matthew Pocket is revealed as the rogue relation. This odd man out, though by no means a perfect father and the head of a most extraordinarily topsy-turvy household (as we discover in stage 2), does at least belong to a world of sanity, one in which the children can map themselves through parental features: he smiles 'with his son's smile' at the beginning of chapter 23, whereas in chapter 13 Miss Havisham is at pains to remind Pip of his alienation from familiar territory when she identifies Joe with scrupulous care as 'the husband of the sister of this boy'.

After he leaves Miss Havisham, Pip wanders through Satis's ruin of a garden again, as he had done in chapter 8, having once more been fed 'in the former dog-like manner' (Estella's attempt to reduce him to the level of the Magwitch who had fed with canine ferocity in chapter 3). Then he looks in at a window and finds himself staring at 'a pale young gentleman'. Unnamed, of course, in this stage of the novel where everything is secret and not yet fully urged beyond the threshold of Pip's unconscious, he is a reflection of Pip in his gentlemanly aspirations. When he asks Pip to fight and suggests 'regular rules' we sense a parody of the two wild beasts of convicts struggling in the marshes. Herbert comes from an untainted non-criminal world and is a gentleman by education and by heart, an amiable testament to a world that operates by 'laws of the game' not only because it can afford to (although moneyless it is nevertheless comfortably bourgeois and stable) but because it is unacquainted with psychological trauma. Magwitch cannot fight 'regular rules', and nobody with Pip's upbringing can really know them either, the novel suggests, for his kind of case-history breeds Barnwell-like murder through the agency of slouching and equally deprived hulks like Orlick.

At this point, remembering Compeyson's public-school background, we see that we have hit the novel's centre of illogicality, that area where Darwin, original sin, Dickens's own autobiography and his zest for fantasy, all mingle and collide. There is no answer, Dickens says, only pattern-weaving, the complex symbolic strands produced by his novel-dreaming self. And so Estella is brought into the problem. The fight makes Pip feel like 'a species of savage young wolf' and Estella demonstrates her complicity in the world represented by that feeling by kissing him. The kiss as a reward for blood shed has a long tradition in the heroic and courtly code, but here it bears witness to her affinity with blood-smeared Smithfield, soiled pound notes, and dead-meat cag-Magwitch. Pip's subsequent covering of Herbert's blood with garden mould (opening of chapter 12) makes him Cain, as we saw earlier; *gentle*men do not murder. And there seem to be insurmountable obstacles to most of us becoming gentlemen in the social sense of the word anyway, for the definition of gentility that the novel teasingly plays with when it presents us with Herbert has rather a lot to do with middle-class comforts and so posits exclusion by really humble birth and the haunting of all *nouveaux* by the stain of their past, which therefore takes on the quality of – and may even be – original sin.

The opening half of stage 1 placed narrative emphasis on Magwitch and proliferated themes of parental loss and binding and enchaining. The second half (chapters 11–19), with chapter 10 as the pivot, focuses on the consequences of an aspect of that binding, Pip's apprenticeship. Although the ceremony in the town hall (chapter 13) is the central episode here, symbolically speaking, the numerically central chapter, 15, is the most significant, for it sees the birth of Orlick, Pip's vengeful double, into the text, and contains *Barnwell* and also the attack on Mrs Joe.

The attack on Mrs Joe is Pip's revenge on his mother for betraying him and, because it implicates Joe, on his father as well. Mrs Joe's lingering state of vegetative incapacity suggests the depth of Pip's brutality to the feminine and also generates another key symbol into the narrative, the hammer. It is a symbol which, despite his rise in fortune, will dominate Pip's later career. As Pip earlier inscribed a message of affectionate loathing for Joe on his slate, so now Mrs Joe inscribes on her slate 'a character that looked like a curious T' (end of chapter 16), a hammer that denotes Orlick (as her attacker and Pip's double) and Pip himself who, as a gentleman in stage 2, will be christened Handel because of the *Harmonious Blacksmith* variations – never, perhaps, realizing that German *Händel* means *trade*.

When Pip walks and talks with Biddy in chapter 17, Orlick pops up again, once more a shadow of Pip, symbolically inseparable from him. And when Jaggers appears in the Three Jolly Bargemen in chapter 18 like the stranger in chapter 10, also 'knowing something secret' but with forefinger rather than file, to offer Pip gentility on behalf of Magwitch, all that happens in consequence is that Pip exchanges his Orlick double for his Drummle double. It is in this chapter, too, that Jaggers's name is first disclosed. Although we do not yet necessarily ponder its significance, we do maybe notice that in this novel of doubles *Jaggers* sounds strangely congruent with *Joe* and *Gargery*: J . . . arger(s); which tells us that in moving into the care of this guardian he is not moving far from his problematic origins at all. Not surprisingly, Pip's own awareness of the difficulty of accommodating his newly found status with what he is only too conscious is his 'real' thick-booted self is signalled by the genesis of a further double, a mocker of the dis-ease he feels in his new and expensive clothes, Trabb's boy (chapter 19).

Stage 2 CHAPTERS 20–39

1. London

The social irony that gentility consists in a quality of heart rather than in a veneer acquired through such accidental externals as birth into a certain class, education, or the benefits of money, confronts Pip forcibly on his arrival in London. Everything that he sees is filthy, criminal, tainted and dark, ominously announcing that his London experiences, culminating as they do in Magwitch's return in chapter 39, echo but do not proceed beyond those endured by Pip in the marsh country of stage 1. There he meditated on death, excluded himself from the forge, and fantasized about gentility. In London he does little more than this as the trappings of gentility enable him to fix his gaze the more firmly on the coldly glittering star that is Estella and that is so opposite to the blazing light and warmth of the forge fire. Meantime, Mrs Pocket is the daughter 'of a certain quite accidental deceased Knight' and relishes the company of Bentley Drummle who is 'actually the next heir but one to a baronetcy' (chapter 23), both of which details remind us how fortuitous, remote and insubstantial a thing gentility is.

The narrative focus on Miss Havisham and Estella continues in stage 2, but the Magwitch interest is displaced on to his agent, Jaggers. Stage 2 also sees the introduction of Wemmick, who complements Herbert as another guide and adviser to Pip. In addition, as a truth-speaker when away from his office he testifies to the split between public and private self that Dickens now saw as inevitable in urban society, and he thus mediates between the novel's concern with obsessional secrecy on the one hand and absolute openness on the other. If the hermetic stranger, pointing with his file to the symbolic father Magwitch and to the dead mother in the form of Miss Havisham, is at the numerical centre of stage 1, then stage 2 focuses at its centre on an even darker reiteration of the same mystery when Pip makes a crucial visit to Miss Havisham and Estella in chapter 29, discovers that Orlick has taken over from him as male hanger-on in the Satis underworld, and then proceeds to visit *Hamlet*.

To return, though, to Pip's entry into London (chapter 20). If we take the Miltonic allusion at the end of stage 1 at its face value, then we know that Pip is once more entering a fallen world; for 'the world lay spread before me' identifies the London that awaits him with the world of death that the expelled Adam and Eve are about to inhabit. But we should note that Pip, even as he stands at the village finger-post at the end of chapter 19 (pastoral equivalent of Jaggers's forefinger), knows where redemption from this world of fallenness and death is to be found – according to the official meaning of the novel, at least:

> Heaven knows we need never be ashamed of our tears, for they are rain upon the blinding dust of earth, overlying our hard hearts. I was better after I had cried, than before – more sorry, more aware of my own ingratitude, more gentle.

Gentle is, as we have seen, the root of Dickens's definition of gentility and the direct opposite of hardness of heart. It is the quality allied to penitence, whose external initial sign is tears which are also the sign of God's grace. By our weeping, 'heaven knows' that we wear away the stone of impenitence and unlovingness and renovate our Adamic self which is made, according to Genesis 2, 'of the dust of the ground'.

The part of London Pip enters is appropriately microcosmic, for Jaggers has his office in Little Britain. Pip is inextricably enmeshed in this 'ugly, crooked, narrow, and dirty' labyrinth of a place because it encapsulates a greater all-embracing social malaise. It is also a reminder of Pip's all-embracing past, for Jaggers practises 'just out of Smithfield, and close by the coach-office'. *Smithfield* intones a familiar and obvious enough message; and so does *coach-office*, speaking as it does in Pip's case not so much of the liberty of travel and hence of escape but, instead, of return journeys by stages that follow psychological as well as geographical terrain and have their morbid epicentres in the boarded stages trodden by the aspiring Wopsle. For confirmation we need only turn, as Pip does, to the coach in which he is conveyed to Jaggers's office, the box of which is 'decorated with an old weather-stained pea-green hammer-cloth'. *Hammer*cloth evokes Orlick and utters the first syllable of the name of the play to which Pip is hurrying, as well as connecting Smithfield with the unfortunately named suburban village inhabited by the Pocket family, Hammersmith.

Another thing that strikes Pip on his all-too-brief ride is how ragged parts of the coach are. It used to belong to an aristocratic family and is ornamented with coronets which function as still visible signs of the shabbiness of gentle blood. The fact that inside it is a combination of straw-yard and rag-shop becomes symbolically significant in the light of the first chapter of stage 3 (chapter 40) when we discover that Pip is now looked after by an old lady and her niece who is like 'an animated rag-bag'. This rag doll displaces the Avenger, the young boy splendidly dressed up in canary waistcoat, cream breeches, and so forth, whom Pip employs in chapter 27 to do nothing except kill time as an emblem of gentility understood in terms of fine clothing and lack of occupation. *Rags*, then, signify an existential truth and fine clothes, as Trabb's boy (the country equivalent of the Avenger) insists by his constant fun-poking, a fabrication. But rags also remind us and Pip of Miss Havisham. They haunt his narrative because he is possessed by the image of his dead mother in her grave-clothes.

He is also haunted by his dead and all-to-absent father; so that his introduction to his new life is through Jaggers's office, and Jaggers, like the real father, Philip Pirrip, is not there. Moreover, the empty office in which Pip waits is distinctly tomblike, recording its status through the repetition of *dismal* – a word brought to its deathly life when we encounter it again in the description of Barnard's Inn in chapter 21 in conjunction with the formal presentation of Wemmick at the beginning of the same chapter as a man who 'appeared to have sustained a good many bereavements'; for *dismals* are, technically, mourning garments. Jaggers's chair, inevitably, is of 'deadly black horse-hair, with rows of brass nails round it, like a coffin'; and the office is as a whole a remarkably patriarchal domain: the words 'master' and 'mastery' resound through the particular paragraph in which the death masks are described; and they in turn, of course, suggest the proximity of those paternal twins, Magwitch and Compeyson. Not surprisingly, therefore, Herbert, infected by the atmosphere, proceeds to attack his front door in chapter 21, as Magwitch assaults his enemy on the marshes, 'as if it were a wild beast'.

The twoness proliferates as Jaggers appears (the death-masks are followed by 'two men of secret appearance', 'two women standing at a corner', and so on), making him the focus of the doubleness in Pip's life because he is the agent of the official world (the Law) as well as the 'confidential agent' (chapter 18) of the underworld in its criminal and deathly senses. Jaggers straddles both sides of the binary divide comprising the notions legal/illegal, living/dead. Shadowy figures and whispering voices accompany him and illicit deals are made on his behalf not just because he is, in his professional capacity, shady, but because he is another threshold figure, a person, like the stranger in chapter 10, mediating between dream and reality, ghosts and fleshly corporeality. With a wonderfully symbolic gesture, Dickens even invests the Law itself with exactly that sense of shifting ambiguity that possesses the whole of Pip's text. For when Pip goes out into the streets he finds that the Lord Chief Justice is for sale – or a view of him is, at any rate – as if he were a 'waxwork', thereby rendering him a grotesquely appropriate partner for that 'ghastly waxwork' Miss Havisham, and making him, too, an extension of Pip's paternal family.

When Pip refuses a peep at the Lord Chief Justice he is offered the gallows instead, which takes us straight back to Magwitch and the hanged pirate; while the 'proprietor' of these goodies, 'an exceedingly dirty and partially drunk minister of justice', is dressed in mildewed clothes that Pip imagines must have been bought cheap from the executioner, a sign that he, too, is a walking testament to the presence of the dead, if not one of the walking dead, and that he is a partner to the Jack of the Causeway in chapter 54. (Note that an alternative word for *jack* is *jagg*, which means 'rags and tatters'; and that a meaning for *Jaggers* as a surname is 'carrier' or 'pedlar': P. H. Reaney, *A Dictionary of British Surnames* (London: Routledge and Kegan Paul, 1958) s.v. *Jaggar*.)

It is in chapter 20 that Pip also first encounters Newgate (it will reappear in chapter 32 when Wemmick guides Pip round it while he is waiting for Estella's coach). Pip meets Mike as well, that fixer of evidence with the 'constitutional cold' who provides a good example of the apparently randomly introduced character who is subsequently absorbed into the novel's symbolic texture. Thus, Mike's cold disappears, metaphorically speaking, into the chest of the Ghost of Hamlet's father in chapter 31, who appears to have had a cough at the time of his death, to have taken it with him to the grave, and to have brought it back again. Even colds in this novel defy elementary physical laws: like Magwitch's clicking throat – a kind of death-rattle – they seem to belong to the world beyond.

Reinforcing the atmosphere, Mike stands in the office like that fatal bellman 'the Bull in Cock Robin pulling at the bell-rope', and telling of death; which means that Jaggers's question to him – 'what is he prepared to swear?' (in connection with the crooked unfortunate who has been found to act the part of 'evidence') – anticipates Magwitch and his demand that Pip and Herbert 'swear' secrecy (chapter 40) and evokes *Hamlet*, I. v, with its paternal Ghost's demand that all swear secrecy concerning his appearance to his son.

59

In this surreal context – the product of Pip's astonishment as he registers London for the first time, but recreated by the older Pip who has experienced it all and is recounting it from the perspective of one who knows what is to come (including the visit to *Hamlet*, Magwitch's return, and so forth) – Mike's admission concerning the 'murderous-looking tall individual' that 'we've dressed him up like—' accuses Pip the well-dressed gentleman, reminds us that murder is a key theme in the novel, and anticipates Magwitch's undisguisable self as it confronts Pip in chapter 40.

2. The Ghost of Barnard *chapters 21–22*

Pip, on his way to the then-fragrant sub-urbanness of Hammersmith to be educated with and by the Pockets, is conducted to Barnard's Inn where he is to lodge with Herbert Pocket. It is, of course, a signal of the psychological repetitiveness of Pip's narrative rather than paucity of invention or mere plot contrivance on Dickens's part that makes this Pocket turn out to be 'the pale young gentleman' of chapter 11. Before Pip reaches Barnard's Inn, however, he has to describe Wemmick, whom he has until now seen only in the gloom of Jaggers's office. When released (unlike Miss Havisham) into 'the light of day', Wemmick displays two notable features. The first is an apparently immobile stone face which later (see chapter 24) develops a post-box slit of a mouth, its rigidity imaging the official self as it enacts its business in a place where routine has parted company from heart. The second is equally striking, for he is wearing elaborate mourning apparel: 'he appeared to have sustained a good many bereavements; for, he wore at least four mourning rings, besides a brooch representing a lady and a weeping willow at a tomb with an urn on it'.

The brooch and one of his rings will be explained later (chapter 24) as having been given by the originals of the death-masks in Jaggers's office. That filling-in of information for Pip's and our inquiring minds is in one way a blind, though; for Wemmick's function as a wearer of ritual mourning is solely to remind Pip of death. He stands at the threshold to Jaggers's office, then as the guide to Barnard's Inn, as another riddling stranger telling of remembrance and the fact of death, thus zooming Pip back – except that he has never escaped from it – to that churchyard of the beginning and to tomblike Satis.

But the information as to the donors of the ring and brooch is, of course, important, for in recalling Magwitch and Compeyson the death-masks reiterate Pip's obsession with his father. Moreover, the details of the brooch – common enough in Victorian funeral iconography – suggest Pip's dead mother, entombed Miss Havisham, and even Molly, dead to Estella and now incarcerated by Jaggers as his housekeeper. As bearer of the emblems of mortality Wemmick, like so many other figures in the novel, straddles two worlds; which means that his two selves – the stony office clerk self and the relaxed private self of his Walworth home – are yet another testament to the novel's binary perception of reality. The Wemmick twins (chapter 48) double Magwitch versus Compeyson and Pip versus Orlick in order to restate the fundamental opposites of outer and inner, body and heart, death and life. Like the stranger with his file and like Jaggers who has the power of life and death over his clients, Wemmick points to the world beyond. It is in that role that he guides Pip to Barnard's Inn.

Historically, Barnard's Inn, in Holborn, was inhabited by lawyers. Originally attached to Gray's Inn, it was now, and had been for a considerable period, a lodging house for gentlemen. In other words, it is another sign of the law's decline, of its appropriation by that law of maximum entropy, the second law of thermodynamics. Over it all hangs 'a frouzy mourning of soot and smoke', which makes it an inanimate effigy of mourning Wemmick. More than that, it tells of ghosts and burials in a descriptive *tour de force* that has at least the psychological brilliance (because they are again predicated upon absence) of Tennyson's 'Mariana' or Browning's 'Childe Roland to the Dark Tower Came'. For Pip discovers that Barnard is a fiction, a disembodied spirit, and his inn to be a dingy collection of shabby buildings.

More subtly, the 'introductory passage' into the 'flat burying-ground' of the square around which the Inn is sited evokes a rite of passage symbolic of Pip's initiation into the dead world of gentility and recapitulatory of the passage through which Pip is led to Miss Havisham. The word *dismal* is scattered here ('dismal trees . . . dismal sparrows . . . dismal cats', etc.) as earlier in connection with Jaggers's office, its deathly meaning amplified by Wemmick's mourning at the beginning of the chapter and the 'mourning of soot' that clothes the place; while the windows with their signs ('To Let To Let To Let') speak once more of absence.

Pip's fantasy of Barnard's avenging soul which needs to be appeased by the 'suicide of the present occupants' compounds the novel's obsession with death and hints at the imminence of *Hamlet* with its obsession with suicide. And when Wemmick says 'the retirement reminds you of the country' he speaks truer than he knows. It isn't just quiet but deathly quiet, a reinscribing on London clay of Pip's marsh country of death, loss, and deprivation. His journey to London has taken him back to Kent.

Once inside the Inn and waiting for Herbert, Pip nearly beheads himself by opening the staircase window, 'for, the lines had rotted away, and it came down like the guillotine'. This is not a gratuitous way of joining the community of Barnard's suicidal inhabitants but, rather, a momentary modulation into the key of *Great Expectations*'s precursor, *A Tale of Two Cities* (1859), the guillotine taking over this once from Pip's favourite gallows. Then when Herbert arrives, he does so like this: 'Gradually there arose before me the hat, head, neckcloth, waistcoat, trousers, boots, of a member of society of about my own standing'. Again, things are more subtle than they might seem. Herbert rises, head first, like a ghost from the underworld, anticipating Magwitch's return in chapter 39 which is first known, like Herbert's arrival, by the sound of 'a footstep on the stair'. But of course the apparition of Herbert's head comes in response to Pip's own near decapitation, as if in this novel of twins and mirror images it is impossible even to lose one's head without somebody bouncing it back.

What, though, of the name *Barnard*? Barnard's Inn was a real place, as we have seen, but that does not prevent Dickens weaving the name into the symbolic fabric of the novel. It contains half of *Barn*well, thus returning Pip the gentleman to his murderous apprenticeship days, as Herbert, too, seems to insist by rechristening him Handel. The 'Harmonious Blacksmith' guarantees that smithies cannot be forgotten however much they might be fragmented and re-formed through variations. But *Handel* itself is even more pernicious. Standing behind the substantial image of the German composer is, as we saw earlier, the meaning of his name, *trade* (readily available to German-oriented mid-nineteenth-century Britain). And, beyond that, lies the verb *händeln*: to deal ill by.

With impeccable imaginative logic Dickens makes Pip endure, at this moment of his realization of his gentility in the form of rotting Barnard, the story of Miss Havisham's life. Arrival in London therefore means another return to the past in the form of the substrate of facts underlying Miss Havisham's behaviour and situation.

3. Inset: The Story of Miss Havisham *chapter 22*

The story will be completed by Magwitch in chapter 42 and by Jaggers in chapter 51. The first time we hear it, though, it is from the lips of a man who cannot benefit from Miss Havisham's will, and has no axe – psychological or other – to grind with her or Estella. Furthermore, unlike Pip, who knows the terror of secrecy, unlike Jaggers, who lives by secrecy, and unlike the stranger of chapter 10, Herbert knows nothing of secrecy. He can expose Miss Havisham's history to Pip, and warn against Estella, because he is open, because he belongs to the world of light, because he is someone who, like Joe, lives at the opposite end of the scale to that dominated by Oedipal darkness and guilt. Herbert tells a tale which means nothing to him in psychological terms. It is his task to articulate the main facts concerning Miss Havisham, to offer an explanation of the riddling and shocking images of bridal decomposition that confronted Pip (and the reader) in stage 1. Yet, on a deeper level, we recall that it is Pip who is retelling Herbert's narrative; and on a deeper level still, that all *Great Expectations*'s words are part of a fiction dreamed by Dickens. Although it functions as an explanation, then, Herbert's story also contains what we might call 'areas of disturbance': words, ideas, situations which in fact reflect and touch upon Pip's (and Dickens's) own problems and uncertainties.

For example, when Herbert says that Miss Havisham's lover, as yet unnamed, was, on his father's authority, 'not to be . . . mistaken for a gentleman', we sense that this says as much about Pip as about Compeyson. Similarly, we suspect that Pip reads his own history into that of Miss Havisham's half-brother Arthur: 'as the son grew a young man, he turned out riotous, extravagant, undutiful – altogether bad. At last his father disinherited him . . .'.

Above all, though, Herbert's narrative confronts Pip with what is in effect a Freudian primal scene that is also a fantasy prohibition: primal scene in that through it Pip is enabled to find his way back to his 'mother' at the moment when she decided to marry the 'father'; fantasy prohibition in that the inset account, like the main narrative, freezes the 'mother' at the point before marriage, keeping her perpetually virginal, 'young', and Oedipally desirable. Seen in this way, it is not Miss Havisham who stopped the clocks so much as

Pip, whose imagination arrests her at the stage where she was about to betray him sexually with the father. Pip then kills the Compeyson-father off, as it were, by making him simply disappear.

Herbert has, says Pip, 'led up to the theme for the purposes of clearing it out of our way', and in a sense he does clear the air: 'we were so much the lighter and easier for having broached it'. But in another way, as I have said, it merely emphasizes the stifling claustrophobia that oppresses Pip's London as it oppresses the 'close' bedroom in the inn near Gravesend in chapter 54 and practically every other place in the novel. For when Pip changes the subject and asks Herbert what he does for a living, Herbert's reply – 'capitalist – and Insurer of Ships' – plunges us into the obsessional abyss once more. *Insurer of ships* in this novel of arklike Hulks and shiplike Satis and returned transport Magwitch who, at the end, sets off down the Thames to catch the Hamburg steamer (what else should it be termed in this text of hammers and *Hamlet*?) is as much as to say 'custodian of the dead', for the waterways of Pip's autobiography are all versions of the Styx, as all its boats are variants on ferryman Charon's.

Capitalist is equally resonant. Those looking at this word as the bridge between trade, business and gentility and, in the mid-century of Marx and Engels, as a clue to Dickens's socialism may, I suspect, be giving Pip too much benefit of the doubt. For to enunciate *capitalist* this near the beginning of the London section is to remind us that we are in the *capital* city, entry to which is, for Pip, guarded by two death-masks in Jaggers's office. If this sounds like ingenious over-reading, we need only remember that Wemmick echoes the word in chapter 24 in the most revealing of contexts: Jaggers is, according to Wemmick, 'deep as Australia' (the current home of Magwitch), to which Pip replies: 'I supposed he had a fine business, and Wemmick said, "Ca-pi-tal!"'; and a few lines later, in reply to Pip's question as to the identity of 'the two odious casts with the twitchy leer upon them', Wemmick explains that they are hanged convicts, getting up as he does so to 'blow . . . the dust off the horrible heads'. This explicitly juxtaposes *capital* against the heads of the hanged men, who are in turn insidiously associated with Pip as Wemmick reveals that one murdered his master, like Pip in his Barnwell persona, and the other, like Pip's shadowy paternal Compeyson, was a forger, 'a gentlemanly Cove' whose speciality was the forging of wills and thus the misdirection of inheritances (which loops back to Compeyson's role in Miss Havisham's story and the temporarily disinherited half-brother Arthur). That Jaggers is 'deep as Australia' makes his mysterious secrecy focus on Magwitch. As a lawyer Jaggers tries to prevent his clients from being hanged, from suffering capitally. When Magwitch returns, 'sea-tossed and sea-washed months and months' (chapter 39; end of stage 2) and, as a returned transport, is under the threat of death by hanging (Dickens misrepresents the legal circumstances slightly to square with the symbolism of the novel), ships and capital come together in a way undreamed of by Herbert in chapter 22 as he tells Miss Havisham's story. (On capital punishment in general in the period, see Philip Collins, *Dickens and Crime* (London: Macmillan, 1962), chapter 10; and on Magwitch's case, p. 281: illegal return from transportation 'had notoriously ceased to be *de facto* capital by the time the action of the novel takes place'.)

But then, of course, Miss Havisham, near the beginning of the novel (chapter 8), as at the end (chapter 49), is imagined by Pip hanging, neck broken, from a beam. Both Pip's symbolic parents are 'hanged men' and the focus of interest is their heads. Jaggers's office, its skylight 'patched like a broken head' (chapter 20), somehow matches Miss Havisham's crazy head to suggest that Pip is proliferating analogues to his own disturbed head. Given the prominence of *Hamlet* at the centre of *Great Expectations*, I should not be surprised if the *capital* puns that link the death of the father with the capital city were prompted by *Hamlet*, III. ii, the exchange between Hamlet and Polonius just before the performance of the inset play:

> *Hamlet*: What did you enact?
> *Polonius*: I did enact Julius Caesar. I was killed i'th' Capitol. Brutus killed me.
> *Hamlet*: It was a brute part of him to kill so capital a calf there.

Wopsle, of course, re-enacts Mark Anthony's oration over the dead Caesar four times a year at the village evening school (chapter 7), and Pip echoes Herbert after Wopsle's *Hamlet* in chapter 31 to tell the man that his performance went 'capitally'.

4. Pip's Adopted Family: Pockets Full of Secrets
see chapter 29

When Herbert names Pip Handel he alliterates his name with his own, again, perhaps, in recognition of the narrative's obligation to *Hamlet* as a parent text; for the name of the play's hero and that of his friend alliterate in companionable reciprocity: Hamlet, Horatio. True to his possible kinship with the rational and faithful Horatio, Herbert is 'frank and easy', the complementary opposite of Pip who, like Horatio to Hamlet, stands outside the nightmare of resurrected fathers and Ophelian bridal mothers. In not being destined for Estella he is destined for sanity, to breathe air that is untainted by the noxious vapours of cag-mag.

This being so, his family doubles Pip's own dead family. Herbert is, in almost all respects that one can enumerate, a positive reflection of Pip, the wholesome opposite of Orlick, Drummle and his other demonic shadows. This does not mean, however, that his family conforms to any normative pattern, for Dickens seems scarcely to have recognized such a phenomenon.

The optimistic feature of Herbert's family is the suggestion it yields that, given some kind of structure revolving around living parents, children manage to tumble themselves up and to survive relatively undamaged into adulthood. The pessimistic inference is that Dickens sees this as a privilege, for *Great Expectations* voices the plight of outcasts, the disinherited sons of Adam. Herbert's chaotic family is, for them, a glimpse of paradise, at the other pole from Miss Havisham's desolate Satis, a re-vision, indeed, of Joe's forge into the ideal because it is tenanted by biological parents and also (Pip's snobbery creeps in and takes over here) because the Pockets are very middle class indeed, soiled by trading connections, perhaps, but uncontaminated by anything worse than that.

Thus Pip, wishing himself to be like the naturally gentlemanly Herbert, whose old clothes look so much more genteel on him than Pip's new ones do on him, adopts the family as his own, finding there mother, father and a large enough number of children at table to compensate for and symbolically replace his own dead parents and siblings. However, a closer look at the Pocket family reveals tensions and ambivalences, a more intimate weaving of it into the darker texture of the novel. Mrs Pocket's lack of interest in looking after her baby locates her in the realm of mother-blame: she is a comic cameo who has somehow been drawn into Pip's web of misogyny; while her 'aristocratic disposition', engendered by her father's knighthood and his conviction that his own father should have been made a baronet, makes her a parody of wealthy Miss Havisham (whose father was a genteel brewer!) and suggests the extent to which Pip accuses his parents, and especially his mother, for not having existed in more wealthy circumstances. In other words, the Mrs Pocket cameo mocks and jests while saying a great deal about Pip's psychology and the snares of snobbery in which he is enwrapped.

The nutcrackering of the baby ('Are infants to be nutcrackered into their tombs?') again, albeit comically, mirrors Pip's memory of Mrs Joe's punitive pins when she bathed him as a child; and Mrs Pocket's constant perusal of the 'book . . . all about titles' points to Pip's quest for parental roots and inheritance. Drummle first appears here, too. He has failed to make it as heir to a title as well, and he is Pip's sinister double in being his malign Orlick self transposed into the world of genteel aspiration (like Orlick, he 'would always creep in-shore like some uncomfortable amphibious creature'; chapter 25).

Drummle awaits Pip at the Pocket household as yet another 'brother', then, just as – on the brighter side – Startop does; though even he arrives accompanied by a caveat against destructive mothers:

Startop had been spoilt by a weak mother and kept at home when he ought to have been at school, but he was devotedly attached to her, and admired her beyond measure. He had a woman's delicacy of feature, and was . . . exactly like his mother. (chapter 25)

It is as if, in this pair, which reduplicates all the text's other pairs (and not least the split Wemmick), Pip meets a further projection of his own dilemma. Startop embodies at once the positive aspect of femininity in the male in contrast to Drummle's utter brutishness, but simultaneously he reflects back at Pip an Oedipal possessiveness which is embarrassing in its overtness.

'Exactly like his mother' also looks poignantly back to the search that was initiated at the beginning of chapter 1 as Pip finally, at the age of seven, realized that his sense of 'the identity of things' depended on his own sense of identity and that that was connected to his awareness of the identity of his parents. The resurrected father

(Magwitch) and mother (Miss Havisham) are part of Pip's attempt to discover how the child is formed by, and belongs to, its parents. Startop, 'exactly like his mother', reminds Pip painfully that unless one has a 'likeness' in the form of a memory image, photograph or painting, one can, if orphaned in infancy, never know who one is 'like'. At this point in Pip's autobiography, then, the search of the orphan is directed at discovering identity through genetically transmitted likeness, a concern with a child's affinity with its biological begetters. When Pip encounters his adoptive family here at Hammersmith (where, as at the forge, the name suggests, shapes and patterns were once formed out of inchoate iron) the motif of genetic inheritance sounds extremely loudly. For Startop as the likeness of his mother has been anticipated at the opening of chapters 23 when Mr Pocket greets Pip 'with his son's smile', and at the end of the chapter Mrs Pocket defines herself as 'grandpapa's granddaughter' as she declares solidarity with the drunken cook who has announced her 'born to be a Duchess'. Likeness matters. It is only someone complacent in their knowledge of their parentage who can say, as Herbert does to Pip, that one would know that Startop was 'exactly like his mother' though one had never seen her.

As Pip settles into the Pocket establishment he gradually meets the other relatives: 'Mr and Mrs Camilla ... Camilla was Mr Pocket's sister. Georgiana, whom I had seen at Miss Havisham's on the same occasion' (chapter 25). Their manifestation of themselves at Hammersmith insists again on the claustrophobic smallness of Pip's universe. In the end the Pockets' house is Satis come to London and this is yet another gathering of Pip's ghostly lost relatives to oversee (or even to overlook) his newly found family.

5. Yet More Pairs: Wemmick and the Aged P.; Jaggers and Molly *chapters 25, 26*

At this point Pip is introduced to another family, as if London were an almost infinitely recessive hall of mirrors reflecting in skewed and less-skewed ways his fascination with kinship structures. This family is Wemmick's, which is housed fairly solidly – and thus in defiance of his motto that property should ideally be portable, an image of the unrooted precariousness of the world of the novel as a whole – in his neo-Gothic castle of a cottage in Walworth.

Wemmick's family consists, though, solely of himself and his father (Miss Skiffins is not yet a member), and his affection and patience for the deaf old man whom he mothers with the deepest love are a positive against which to measure the father hatred which has been the novel's norm up to this point; so that even before Pip visits *Hamlet* we sense that Wemmick's castle is a 'right' form of Elsinore, and his relationship with his Aged P. a counter image to Hamlet's with his dead father and Pip's to his.

Yet it might also be said that Wemmick's father is imprisoned; that his son is a benign despot over the man who begot him. The detail of the firing of the gun at nine o'clock each night reinforces the impression by glancing back at entombed Miss Havisham, stuck in expectation at twenty to nine and (for Dickens was never careless of symbolic detail) anticipating that other prison, the sluice-house, where, in the mist and darkness, at nine p.m., Pip will encounter Orlick. Maybe, then, Wemmick the builder and maintainer of the castle and its garden does not 'brush ... the Newgate cobwebs' as completely away as he would wish. Maybe they touch him almost as firmly as they touch Pip, Estella and the Drummle spider, so that when he describes himself 'my own Jack of all Trades' we see vistas of shamingly misnamed playing cards, the Jack of the Causeway, and Jaggers, from whom Wemmick parts in the evening only to rejoin in the morning as if he and the Aged P. were the termini of his existence, the lords (to appropriate a phrase used most recently by Geoffrey Hill) of his limits.

In confirmation of the all-embracingness of Jack-Jaggers, chapter 26 takes Pip straight to Jaggers's house in Gerrard Street, Soho, but only after Jaggers has washed his hands, like Pilate, of his criminal clientele and wiped them on 'an unusually large jack towel'. The house is grand, dirty and unkempt, like Satis in its gloom and stately decay, like Barnard's Inn in its dirty windows and desolation. Whereas Wemmick's castle contained an Aged P. of a father, however, Jaggers's house conceals, like Satis, a female secret in the form of Molly the housekeeper. Molly, for whose appearance Wemmick has prepared Pip in the previous chapter ('you'll see a wild beast tamed') is the forcibly constrained equivalent of Miss Havisham: strong, sullen, mysterious, child-abandoning, conceivably mad and scarred with bramble scratches she simultaneously encodes all Pip's mother-hatred and focuses Dickens's fundamental problem with civilization: that it is little more than a necessary yet unsuccessful restraint on humanity's instinctive brutality.

Molly also stands as a mute witness, like Mrs Joe and Miss Havisham in their different ways, to the history of female oppression. For if Jaggers is, as I suggested earlier, another manifestation of Pip's concern with the father as prohibitor, his taming of Molly by force and his retention of her by emotional blackmail are the signs and forms of marital domination. As Wemmick is to the Aged P., the faithful son who yet, in my darkly deconstructive reading of the text at any rate, keeps that inanely smiling and vacant father a prisoner in his castle, so is the Jaggers husband to Molly. She serves him and he patronizes her. At this point Dickens's awareness of the hypocrisies of a social structure built on the subservient female cuts across the Oedipal fantasies he releases in *Great Expectations* on Pip's behalf. Molly as the tamed beast is, momentarily at least, a crude paradigm of the process imposed on any woman who hopes to succeed in Victorian marriage (we remember what Drummle does to Estella).

Moreover, through her name – a familiar form of Mary – Molly evokes the Virgin Mary, biblical rerun of Eve, the immaculate woman who displaces the maculate cause of our Fall. She therefore complements Eve-like Miss Havisham, as the briar-marks quietly insist, since thorns were one of the consequences of the Fall (Genesis 3:18). Pip idolizes women and hates them simultaneously, in familiar patriarchal fashion. Maybe we do not need to be reminded, then, that a 'moll' is also a 'prostitute'.

Pip records his fascination with Molly in the same chapter (26) when, admitting her uncanniness, he notes: 'I always saw in her face, a face rising out of the caldron' and then remarks that 'years afterwards, [he] made a dreadful likeness of' her with the aid of another woman and 'a bowl of flaming spirits in a dark room'.

71

Molly is, by this account, the ghost of his mother in yet another form mediated through Pip's experience of seeing *Macbeth* 'a night or two before' and brooding on 'the faces [Pip] had seen rise out of the Witches' caldron'. Miss Havisham is a witch, of course ('the Witch of the place'), so that Molly's face is at once a reflection of hers and a window into the *Macbeth* cauldron as yet another repository of the novel's secrets. For the witches' cauldron contains, like *Great Expectations* itself, 'sow's blood . . . [and] grease, that's sweaten/From the murderer's gibbet' and produces images of heads, children and a show of patriarchal kings that announces a line of inheritance that Pip would dearly (like Macbeth) love to be included in.

Pip's speculation about Molly's diseased heart on the same page links her in addition – though perhaps merely through an arbitrary verbal sign – to broken-hearted and stone-hearted Miss Havisham and Estella.

6. Joe's Journey and Pip's Return *chapters 27–30*

After these parental configurations, Joe returns into the novel as a challenge to what Biddy calls Pip's 'good heart' and as a test of Pip's gentle-manliness (opening of chapter 27). Superficially, Joe's visit functions to bring the message from Miss Havisham that Estella is home from finishing school and that she would be glad to see Pip. It also shows Pip's snobbishness, what he calls his 'keen sense of incongruity' between Joe and his London self. More profoundly, signals are generated by the fact that Joe has visited the 'Blacking Ware'us' (which, even if it isn't the Warren's Blacking of Dickens's childhood nevertheless evokes its black secret) and that he has attended a performance of *Hamlet*, which prompts in its turn the utterance of the novel's deepest and most heartfelt question, touching as it does not only Pip's history but Joe's as well: 'Which I meantersay, if the ghost of a man's own father cannot be allowed to claim his attention, what can, Sir?' (chapter 27) – a question, incidentally, which Pip does not answer.

Joe's 'good honest face all glowing and shining' reveals that he is the loving father Pip is looking for all along; but his innocent bearing of the tidings of Hamlet and the Ghost shows us, as readers, that he is walking Quixote-like through a world of threatening signs: Barnard is 'shedding sooty tears outside' in lamentation for the dead who inhabit his graveyard of an inn as well as for his ghostly self; and Pip allows Joe to be greeted by the smartly dressed and useless Avenger who 'haunt[s his] existence'.

In other words, Joe's arrival in London is so ominous with ghosts that the boy even gains the additional description of the 'avenging phantom'. As we have seen, he is the London equivalent of Trabb's boy, a superbly comic parody of Pip's sartorial vanities (his real name, Pepper, suggests the constant punishment and battering his presence aims at Pip). Equally, however, he reminds us how deeply rooted *Great Expectations*, like *Hamlet*, is in the revenge tradition, ostensibly in preparation for Pip's return to Miss Havisham and Estella and their lives of sworn vengeance on men, and also as a reminder that Pip's life, too, is ghosted by the torments of revenge. Yet Joe, like so many comic inventions, is free. He can and does walk away from Pip's psychological prison, unharmed by the malevolences it directs at him. And before he does so he is given one of the funniest, as well as one of the most resonant, lines in the novel when he voices his confidential opinion of Barnard's Inn: 'I wouldn't keep a pig in it myself . . .'.

Joe's London visit, then, draws Pip back to Miss Havisham (chapters 28, 29), but his snobbery makes the prodigal pig from Barnard's Inn ignore the hospitality of the forge and put up at the Blue Boar instead. Chapter 28 itself is devoted to the journey down, a brilliantly symbolic – almost hallucinatory – narrative moment which reminds us again how closely Pip lives alongside his unconscious, how quickly he drops back into the world of that childhood nightmare when Magwitch leaped at him from among the tombstones.

I follow Joe's lead (chapter 27) in using the word *drop* here. He reveals that Wopsle has 'had a drop', which of course means a decline in professional standing but, in this text of unstable signifiers, with its Gerrard Street noose-like swags, its death-masks, its hanged pirate and hanged Miss Havisham, it evokes death by hanging and the sickening release of the trap door under the condemned man's feet, not to mention the trap-door through which Old Hamlet enters the cellarage (*Hamlet*, I. v). The phrase released by Joe in chapter 27 thus waits to descend on Pip in the following chapters, for Pip, as it were, drops straight into his past in chapter 28 when he catches his coach and finds that there are 'two convicts going down with [him]'. Rejected and despised, monuments to that Darwinian and Adamic past that society tries to conceal from itself ('lower animals . . . a most disagreeable and degraded spectacle'), they recall the Magwitch-Compeyson twins and then literally resurrect Pip's childhood when one of them turns out to be the stranger from chapter 10. He sits behind Pip on the coach, 'his breath on the hair of [Pip's] head', as Compeyson will sit, ghostlike and unacknowledged, behind Pip at the pantomime in chapter 47, witnessing the fact that what these convicts represent in Pip's life is as inescapable as the air he breathes. As he tells of the marshes and of the two one-pound notes, we are not really sure whether we are overhearing dream or reality, for to Pip here both seem to be the same. He has dozed off (dropped off, we might say) and, according to him, wakened to the marshy breath of his home countryside; but waking and dreaming are for Pip undifferentiated events because 'The very first words I heard them interchange as I became conscious were the words of my own thought, "Two One Pound notes."'

After Pip has left the coach his 'fancy' recalls the image of 'the wicked Noah's Ark', an indication that his return is as much psychological as topographical; so that when he describes Estella in chapter 29 as Satis's 'princess' whom it is his task to rescue and marry, the romance motif reinforces the element of repressive fantasy, making Estella the buried secret lying at the heart of all those stopped clocks. She is 'irresistible', her beauty the 'clue' (umbilical thread) directing us to her presence at the centre of Pip's 'poor labyrinth'. Pip's awareness of the fact that he is engaged on a chronological journey back to retrieve his mother as a girl is suggested by the ambiguity of 'I so shaped out my walk as to arrive at the gate *at my old time*' (my italics).

He is met by Orlick, who has left the forge to become Satis's porter where he inhabits a room 'not unlike the kind of place usually assigned to a gate-porter in Paris' – an innocent enough detail were it not for the guillotine in chapter 21 and the fact that Estella is just back from France, which make it seem that the world of *A Tale of Two Cities* is pressing rather close with its *tricoteuses* and its ominously revolutionary mob. Orlick's newly acquired expletive, 'Burn me, if I know!', makes him one of the suffering damned welcoming Pip back into that tormented psychological space which he has reserved for his mother understood as the combined figure of Estella and Miss Havisham (the 'Miss Est-Havisham' of chapter 15).

Orlick hits the bell with a hammer and Pip walks off down the passage he trod years ago in his 'thick boots' to find the two women in that 'dreamy room' which releases in Pip awareness of his own primal guilt, obligations and betrayal: 'it was impossible to dissociate [Estella's] presence from ... all those ill-regulated aspirations that had first made me ashamed of home and Joe – from all those visions that had raised her face in the glowing fire'. As the impulse behind Pip's urge to reject Joe, Estella is, of course, inseparable from Miss Havisham. This passage, in its insistence that 'it was impossible for [Pip] to separate her ... from the innermost life of [his] life', records the abiding call of the mother, always young and beautiful, to Pip, and in its recollection of the face in the fire recalls Molly's face in the cauldron. Molly and Estella, mother and daughter, are thus reconciled in two hauntingly visionary moments, fused as the ultimate goal or *telos* of Pip's quest.

Estella next becomes his lady of the garden as they walk outside, its rankness figuring all the obstacles lying in the path of his

75

aspiration to her. Moreover, she now bears the ghostly memory trace of her mother's (*the* mother's) hand in another moment of the undeniable uncanny. In other words, in this particular plunge into the past the further clue is released that Estella is 'knowable' to Pip – recognizable to him as the beloved she is – by virtue of her affinity with something he as yet fails to fully recognize but will eventually know to be Molly: Magwitch's wife, sensed by her hand as it is reduplicated in that of her daughter by the boy who was brought up *by hand* by his sister doubling for the dead mother. Molly approached by this route appears as the primal mother in the palimpsest that is Pip's autobiography, containing as it does multiply inscribed and reinscribed hieroglyphs of the same thing. She seems to lie further back in Pip's history than Miss Havisham herself. Yet anteriority is not really in question. All Pip's mothers are, psychologically speaking, synchronous, and iterations of Georgiana, interred as she is from the novel's beginning in her grave and in Pip's memory. It is a sign of the depths that are being plumbed here that the full connection is made apparent only at the end when, in chapter 58, Pumblechook discloses more than the tombstone does: 'This is him untoe the sister of which I was uncle by marriage, as her name was Georgiana M'ria from her own mother, let him deny it if he can!' Molly (familiar form of Mary) *is* Georgiana M'ria. But the reader interested in the way fiction ghosts autobiography will also sense that the long elegiac cry that is *Great Expectations* encodes a lament – forms indeed an epitaph for – all Dickens's own lost female beloveds: for Maria Beadnell, whom he adored but who rejected him and who finds her way into Estella; for his dead sister-in-law Mary Hogarth who died at the age of seventeen, from whose death he never recovered, and whose ring he wore until his own death over thirty years later; and for Georgina Hogarth, another sister-in-law and a favourite one who actually outlived him but who was associated in his mind with death because of her likeness to Mary. Her resemblance to Mary is so 'strong' and 'so strange a one, at times, that when she and Kate [Mrs Dickens] and I are sitting together, I seem to think that what has happened is a melancholy dream from which I am just awakening' (letter to Mrs Hogarth quoted in Edgar Johnson, *Charles Dickens: His Tragedy and Triumph*, abridged edn (Allen Lane, 1977), chapter 22).

The presence of Jaggers in this chapter, known first by the scent of his soap rather than by sight (so that he is an uncanny presence too), admits paternal prohibition into this scene as he had done in chapter 11. He cross-questions Pip and controls the card game at the end of the chapter with patriarchal arrogance, a Jack of a Jaggers who has jumped out of the card games of Pip's yesterdays: 'What I suffered from, was the incompatibility between his cold presence and my feelings towards Estella'. The game breaks up – as it would have to in this novel – at nine p.m. in order to release Pip back to London and the performance of *Hamlet* in which he will see a king and queen – not Queen Havisham ('you kiss my hand as if I were a queen'; chapter 29) or cardboard kings and queens – act out in rather eccentric form his Oedipal fantasies. Just before that, however, Herbert clears the air, as Joe had tried to in chapter 27, by offering a counter-image to Pip's claustrophobic involvement in Miss Havisham and Estella. For Herbert is engaged to a girl called Clara (chapter 30).

Yet even this apparently simple item of news has its ramifications for the brooding Pip. Clara is subject to a tyrannical father whom Herbert has not seen – nor ever will see – a former ship's purser or supplier of provisions who lives in 'his room overhead' in a lodging house near the river. His death will liberate Clara as a reminder that Pip's own dead father should have had a place in his memory but should not have been allowed to tyrannize over and deform his life. The abrupt departure of Pip to *Hamlet* suggests how crucial a figure old Bill Barley is. The fact that he is a purser confirms it. When Magwitch returns after his long sea voyage he will adopt the name of Provis, the provi-der, supplier of provisions of gentility to Pip, Pip's own Bill Barley who must be endured to his death.

7. *Hamlet* at the Centre *chapter 31*

Although Pip arrives at Denmark at the opening of chapter 31 he has, in a sense, been there all along. For the inclusion of *Hamlet* in his autobiography invites us to re-read its characters and topography in terms of Shakespeare's play; or, more precisely, to realize that they have been readable in terms of *Hamlet* from the beginning. Thus, Magwitch leaping out from the tombstones must indeed be 'the ghost of [Pip's] own father' (chapter 27) as a forbidding rerun of Old Hamlet's ghost; Satis's rank garden is inevitably a reflection of Denmark; Miss Havisham cannot but be an aged Ophelia, and so on. Furthermore, *Hamlet* defines Pip's relationship with Herbert by anticipating it in Hamlet's with Horatio, and, as I have suggested, it may even be that *Hamlet* is the secret underlying one of the novel's main symbols, that of the hammer, which, every time it is mentioned, insists through its initial syllable on the dominating presence of Shakespeare's play in Pip's text.

The first thing to be said about Wopsle's *Hamlet* is that it is, as described by Pip, extremely funny. The second is that it concentrates on only a few episodes and characters: the ghost scenes in Act I, the Queen and Ophelia, the suicide soliloquy in Act III, and the churchyard in Act V. As a comic reading of the play it releases the psychological and narrative tension that has been gradually increasing in the novel and has just peaked with the latest encounter with Miss Havisham and Estella. Wopsle's *Hamlet* displays actors involved in handling and mishandling themes that are of the profoundest relevance to Pip, and getting laughs from an anarchically appreciative audience out for a good time. Simultaneously, though, we must recognize that it is Pip the narrator who is our interpreter on this, as on all other, occasions: the comic *Hamlet*, then, identifies the older, retrospective, narrating Pip's tone of voice once and for all as perceptively ironic, humorously aware, and distanced from his darker self. Even though, as I shall argue, Pip can never escape the Oedipal bind in which he is entrapped, his voice rises above it, describing wittily even while he is still suffering, acknowledging that for most of his readers his problems are not their own and that for many of them they may even be incomprehensibly farcical.

The incidents selected from the play underline these points. Pip first remembers the ghostly father, whose derisive greeting from the audience, itself clearly not suffering either individually or *en masse* from grief over fathers long since or recently dead, neatly and salutarily places for us as readers the whole burden of Pip's narrative in so far as it concerns the grave of Pip's own father, Magwitch in all his terror in the churchyard at the beginning, Jaggers in his grave of an office, and so on. Yet the comic *Hamlet* also rephrases Pip's obsessions in a more sombre way, too. Thus, the 'very buxom' Gertrude, christened 'the kettledrum' by the audience, mirrors his omnivorous appetite for mothers, as the Ghost reflects his commitment to dead fathers. This fat mother is satisfyingly maternal in contrast to spiky Mrs Joe, bramble-scratched Molly, and hag-ridden Miss Havisham. The focus on madness (Ophelia's; Hamlet's as he carefully arranges the disorder of his stockings) raises a question about the aetiology of lunacy and its external signs that is central to the novel. The suicide soliloquy (III. i) – over which, according to Pip, 'quite a Debating Society arose' – focuses on what is the most basic problem in *Great Expectations* as in *Hamlet* itself: the status of the dead in relation to the living, and the nature of that ultimate unknown, 'the undiscovered country from whose bourn/No traveller returns' (except that Magwitch does); the quality of that 'sleep of death' and its dreams which Miss Havisham and Magwitch are living out before us. This soliloquy picks up the theme of Hamlet's first soliloquy in I. ii:

> O that this too too solid flesh would melt,
> Thaw, and resolve itself into a dew!
> Or that the everlasting had not fixed
> His canon 'gainst self-slaughter . . .

It also contains the play's earliest description of the world as an 'unweeded garden'. In other words, Wopsle's Hamlet defines Miss Havisham's Satis as the site of absolute despair, one which by definition (because he is its conceiver and narrator) labels Pip a despairing melancholic who must, inevitably, near the end of the novel, struggling with his dark cacodaemon in the form of Orlick, actually contemplate a Hamlet-like vision of his own death in the sluice-house while it is embraced by 'the choking vapour of the kiln' (chapter 53). As Orlick swigs from his bottle, threatening death, Pip says:

I knew that every drop it held, was a drop of my life. I knew that when I was changed into a part of the vapour that had crept towards me but a little while before, like my own warning ghost, he would ... make all haste to town.

As Pip stands on the brink of his own grave, then, he becomes Hamlet contemplating the 'resolving' of his flesh into droplets, and then the Hamlet of chapter 31's churchyard with Orlick as his Laertes, 'on the brink of the orchestra and the grave', as if his life is inconceivable without invocation of the *Hamlet* paradigm.

Pip in the grave with Orlick-Laertes is Pip confronting the horror that has haunted him since he became aware of the dreadful secret of parental death contained in the graves in chapter 1. He has walked the catacombs of Satis; he has gazed at Jaggers's coffin of a chair. Now, finally, he 'dies' as he imagines his body dissolving into vapour droplets. This 'death' arises from an absolute confrontation with his dark self, the self which hated Mrs Joe and despised Joe: in fact, the self which did and thought all the things that Orlick accuses it of.

But, of course, this confrontation can be traced back through the novel to Pip's confrontation with Herbert, Joe's with Orlick (chapter 15), and Compeyson's with Magwitch in chapter 5. It is as if the primal pair Abel and Cain, redefined by *Hamlet* into Old Hamlet and Claudius (Claudius's 'my offence is rank, it smells to heaven;/It hath the primal eldest curse upon it;/A brother's murder!' in III.iii; Hamlet's 'Look here, upon this picture, and on this;/The counterfeit presentment of two brothers' in the following scene) and then modulated, as they are in the play, into Hamlet-Laertes, proceed to define the narrative movement of *Great Expectations* as constant struggle and opposition. By this criterion Wopsle's performance does indeed go 'capitally, capitally' (Pip echoing Herbert in chapter 31) because it activates those couples whose most uncanny emblem in the novel is the pair of heads in Jaggers's office, the hanged men whom Pip, with the noose about his neck in the sluice-house in chapter 53, is within an inch of joining.

Beyond the farce, then, *Hamlet* proposes a riddling clue to the meaning of *Great Expectations* as a novel of self pitted against self in a struggle based on guilt in relation to the dead father which is in turn connected to the way Pip imagines his mother: as an object of love who is also hated, Eve-like, for her betrayal of him by causing him to fall, through her death, into the desolation of his orphaned babyhood. The comic performance enables Pip to take the skeletons out of his family cupboard and dust them over, as Wopsle does his fingers after touching the skull, even to posit that there may be no skeletons after all (the coffin on stage is palpably empty). But Pip's unconscious knows that the comic reading of Shakespeare's text is a blind, for he goes 'miserably' to bed afterwards to dream of marriage and then of 'play[ing] Hamlet to Miss Havisham's Ghost' in an extraordinary reversal of sexual and familial roles that tells us exactly how Oedipal Pip's fantasy about his mother is.

8. From *Hamlet* back to Satis *chapters 32–38*

The last chapters of stage 2 lead remorselessly to the fact of Magwitch's return and assume a more sober tone after the exuberances of the *Hamlet* chapter. The narrative *motif* of this group of chapters is again return to the past, a past of which Magwitch will, as 'the ghost of [Pip's] own father', inevitably emerge. Thus, Estella's arrival in London in order that she may reside with a family in Richmond is preceded by a visit to Newgate which reenacts in expanded form Pip's tour on his arrival in London and, more important, exposes his symbolic – and Estella's actual – roots in Molly's and Magwitch's criminal selves (the prison is, as it were, the primal scene for both of them as, in the shape of the Marshalsea, it was the scene of primal shame to Dickens). In this connection it is worth recalling that in his essay 'Where We Stopped Growing' (*Household Words*, 1 January 1853), which examines those childhood moments, beliefs and memories which are so central to our formation that we never outgrow them (they are, in effect, Wordsworthian spots of time), Dickens moved from describing the 'White Woman' of Berners Street, old, simpering and in her bridal dress (one of the prototypes for Miss Havisham) straight on to 'the rugged walls of Newgate' (Dickens, *Miscellaneous Papers*, intro. P. J. M. Scott, 2 vols (Kraus Reprint, New York, 1983), vol. I, p. 389).

The Richmond house, like Satis, is a memorial to the dead, though more a testament to the processes of history than the voluntary suicide of a deranged Miss Havisham (chapter 33). Estella slips into it nevertheless, as into Satis, like a ghost, to become symbolically at one with the past as Miss Havisham herself is, and towards the end of the chapter the 'grave' pun sounds again when, after mentioning the 'great procession of the dead', Pip pauses over the 'bell with an old voice [which] sounded gravely in the moonlight' as if reminding himself of the extent to which the characters of his autobiography inhabit the timeless world of his unconscious where the dead are constantly mummified. And when he tells us how he 'haunted Richmond' (in chapter 34 as also in an agonized paragraph at the beginning of chapter 38) he is, I think, telling us less about the desperations of the lovesick – though Dickens's passion for Ellen Ternan clearly sounds through here – than he is about his acknowledgement of his Hamlet-like kinship with the world of the dead.

Then, as Magwitch approaches ever nearer, Pip literally plunges into a grave that is also the grave of memory with Mrs Joe's death: 'It was the first time that a grave had opened in my road of life, and the gap it made in the smooth ground was wonderful' (chapter 35). Her death enables him to return to his true home in fact and in memory, to move beyond Satis back to the forge and, in a moment of romantic epiphany (as in Wordsworth again, or Nelly Dean's visionary gleam of Hindley at the beginning of *Wuthering Heights*, chapter 11), to admit Mrs Joe as the mother she really was to him:

It was fine summer weather again, and, as I walked along, the times when I was a little helpless creature, and my sister did not spare me, vividly returned. But they returned with a gentle tone upon them that softened even the edge of Tickler.

The chapter is elegiac and emotionally just right (except perhaps to a radical feminist reader of Pip's text) in its simply paratactic report of Mrs Joe's dying words and actions, mediated as they are through Biddy:

'She made signs to me that she wanted [Joe] to sit down close to her, and wanted me to put her arms round his neck. So I put them round his neck, and she laid her head on his shoulder quite content and satisfied. And so she presently said "Joe" again, and once "Pardon," and once "Pip." And so she never lifted her head up any more, and it was just an hour later when we laid it down on her own bed, because we found she was gone.'

It is as if the performance of *Hamlet*, with its opened tomb of Act I and its open grave in Act V, has enabled Pip to permit Mrs Joe finally to die (his memory has held her in a vegetative limbo for a frighteningly large number of years); as if it has permitted him to recognize the need of the dead to be allowed to rest. Mrs Joe's death functions, therefore, as a symbolic erasure of Pip's hatred, love, and all the other mixed up emotions that are connected with his dead mother and that led to the generation of Miss Havisham and Estella. It is of the utmost importance that he should hear of her last moments, hear that she died well and peacefully, because that knowledge supplies a searing gap in his knowledge of Georgiana, his 'real' mother, who died, so far as he is aware, voiceless in his infancy.

Yet although the death and funeral function ritually as a recognition and farewell, they do not in fact lay to rest Pip's larger and deeper fears, which remain embodied in the figures of Miss Havisham and Magwitch. Indeed, the grave that opens in Pip's road of life (not the first, of course, since his parents' were that) actually reactivates the fears generated by his dead mother and father. Miss Havisham becomes more ghostly and terrible, a tormented phantom (chapter 38); and Magwitch himself appears (chapter 39) heralded by apocalyptic portents (storm, flood and wind 'like discharges of cannon' that takes us back to the guns fired on his escape from the Hulks and the cannon fired from the Elsinore battlements in *Hamlet*'s Act I). And as the opening of chapter 39 reveals, even Mrs Joe herself has not really been laid to rest after all: 'I heard a footstep on the stair. What nervous folly made me start, and awfully connect it with the footstep of my dead sister, matters not.' However, it *does* matter because this is a further clue that the inhabitants of Pip's autobiography are all ghostly duplicates of each other. Those of us interested in pursuing the involuted complexities of Pip's habit of doubling even further might also note the way in which 'the figure of my sister in her chair by the kitchen fire' (opening of chapter 35) is a transformation of Pip's opening description of the *Hamlet* performance ('On our arrival in Denmark, we found the king and queen of that country elevated in two arm-chairs on a kitchen table') as well as being an anticipation of Miss Havisham's death by fire in chapter 49.

This confirms what I suggested at the beginning of this study, that many of Pip's experiences, however spaced through the narrative in a sequence dictated by the causality of plot and the demands of chronology, are nevertheless, psychologically speaking, identical and, in effect, synchronous. Hence, again, at the beginning of chapter 36, when Pip attains his twenty-first birthday and 'comes of age', he imagines himself back into his seven-year-old self in chapter 1. It is November, the month of All Souls and so of the spirits of the dead, the month in which Frankenstein completed work on his creature (*Frankenstein*, chapter 5), and Pip finds himself facing Jaggers in his office:

'Take a chair, Mr Pip,' said my guardian.
As I sat down, and he preserved his attitude and bent his brows at his boots, I felt at a disadvantage, which reminded me of that old time when I had been put on a tombstone. The two ghastly casts on the shelf were not far from him, and their expression was as if they were making a stupid apoplectic attempt to attend to the conversation.

Jaggers takes on the role of Magwitch while, as his agent, he is acting on Magwitch's (paternal) authority. His position in relation to Pip signals the answer, uncannily, to Pip's question at the very moment he is telling Pip nothing except that he will know more when he is 'in communication with the fountain-head'. The two listening casts – audience to this colloquy between father and son – silently affirm, as Jaggers's authoritarian posture does too, that 'the fountain-head' has more than a little connection with Magwitch and that tombstone of long ago; and the visit to Wemmick (chapter 37; ostensibly to discover his Walworth sentiments as to how Pip can help Herbert financially) reinforces Pip's sense that the answer to his question 'who is my benefactor?' is really 'your mother and father'. For the castle with its Aged P. – animated enough to be engaged in conversation this time – reflects back on Jaggers and Pip and Wopsle's Elsinore and prepares Pip for his return to Satis in chapter 38, itself a prelude to Magwitch's return in the following chapter.

Chapter 38, the last occasion when Pip can still feel that Miss Havisham is his benefactor and Estella intended for him by her, is remarkable largely for the heightened way in which it depicts Miss Havisham and for the level of self-awareness Pip displays in narrating it. From his imagining of his future ghostly haunting of Estella's Richmond house to his account of Miss Havisham's witchlike and spectral qualities, intenser now than they were earlier in chapters 8 and 11, his perceptions take on the colouring of fevered hallucinations as he approaches the central secret of his history, the revelation of Magwitch's identity. Then, when he turns from Miss Havisham to the room itself, to examine it as if for the first time since he saw it in chapter 8, he suddenly stands back from the hallucination, his conspiracy with the necrophiliac compartment within his imagination:

As I looked round at [the candles], and at the pale gloom they made, and at the stopped clock, and at the withered articles of bridal dress upon the table and the ground, and at her own awful figure with its ghostly reflection thrown large by the fire upon the ceiling and the wall, I saw in everything the construction that my mind had come to, repeated and thrown back to me. My thoughts passed into the great room across the landing where the table was spread, and I saw it written, as it were, in the falls of the cobwebs from the centre-piece, in the crawlings of the spiders on the cloth, in the tracks of the mice as they betook their little quickened hearts behind the panels, and in the gropings and pausings of the beetles on the floor.

85

These are among the most important sentences in the novel, for they mean much more than that Pip begins to suspect the illusory nature of his Satis quest, that it is in the end a grasping after shadows. They say that Pip recognizes the extent to which he has constructed his own reality; and that his autobiography – his writing of his life in the form of the text *Great Expectations* – is a testament to his preoccupation with the inscribing of death and decay and to his fantasy of himself as the Spider-like Drummle double (Jaggers christens Drummle in chapter 26). They reveal, too, that Miss Havisham is 'the construction that [his] mind' created when he saw his mother's grave, a construction that mirrors his vision back at him just as Magwitch is reflected back at him from his longing gaze at the paternal tombstone. The paragraph demonstrates once more the extent to which Pip, like George Eliot's Mr Casaubon a few years later (*Middlemarch*, chapter 10), walks too much in vaults, constructing his own images and texts of the dead.

Introduced as it is by this paragraph, the dialogue that Pip then records between Miss Havisham and Estella ('the first time I had ever seen them opposed') tells us less about their relationship as adoptive mother and daughter than it does about Pip himself. He is, surely, acting out through Estella an imagined revenge scenario with his own mother, punishing her for that unforgivable error she made all those years ago by dying and abandoning her infant. Part of the exchange reads:

'You stock and stone!' exclaimed Miss Havisham. 'You cold, cold heart!'

'What?' said Estella, preserving her attitude of indifference . . . 'do you reproach me for being cold? You?'

'Are you not?' was the fierce retort.

'You should know,' said Estella. 'I am what you have made me . . .'

'O look at her, look at her!' cried Miss Havisham, bitterly; 'Look at her, so hard and thankless, on the hearth where she was reared! Where I took her into this wretched breast when it was first bleeding from its stabs . . .'

The logic of the dialogue seems to run as follows: the child (Estella substituting for Pip) has been formed in the image of the mother – cold, heartless, stonelike – because the mother is dead (cold as her gravestone, her heart corrupted). There is perhaps a pun floating around in Pip's mind on *stock*: here not just a stupid person or blockhead but, as the stock or trunk of a tree, a word applied to the originator of a family or race (*Oxford English Dictionary*, s.v. *stock* sb. 1, I. 3). The child is, in effect, a zombie (the *Frankenstein* echoes begin to sound clearly here, I think), chillingly taunting the mother as it sees its chance of revenge for its non-upbringing. I suspect that Mrs Joe is resurrected, too, to become once again the victim of Pip's fury: for isn't Miss Havisham's stabbed and lacerated breast Pip's visitation on Miss Havisham of Mrs Joe's loathed 'impregnable bib . . . stuck full of pins and needles' (chapter 2) with which she covered her unmaternal breast? Pip has turned the bib round to give Miss Havisham (through Compeyson) the most appalling wounds with it.

The confrontation ends with Estella stitching one of Miss Havisham's disintegrating bridal vestments which reminds him of 'the faded tatters of old banners that I have seen hanging up in cathedrals', and so of the skeleton in its 'ashes of a rich dress' exhumed from under a church pavement in chapter 8, with its own reminder of the extent to which Pip conceives of Miss Havisham as his disinterred mummy of a mother. When he tries to sleep he is haunted by her, and when he gets up he watches her, literally, walk: 'going along . . . in a ghostly manner, making a low cry . . . unearthly by candle light'. She *is* his mother, *unearthly* because escaped from her interment in the grave, and the 'mildewed air of the feast-chamber' which is to be her death chamber is therefore that of an opened grave. Ghostly Miss Havisham in her tormented prowlings leads Pip straight to the presence of Magwitch, back from the grave himself again in chapter 39.

9. Magwitch's Return *chapters 39–40*

Magwitch's return actually spans the end of stage 2 (chapter 39) and the opening of stage 3 (chapter 40). The fact of his return governs and dominates the remainder of the novel. It is here (chapter 40) that he is named as Abel and, through that naming, known for what he is, the dead (symbolically murdered) father come back, to be confronted, accommodated and accepted so that he may, finally, be laid to rest in the grave from which he emerged into the novel in chapter 1. The significance of Magwitch's second appearance is that it suggests that Pip, like all of us perhaps, understands certain phenomena differently at different stages of his life. The irruption of this ghostly father when Pip was a child was so horrifying and intolerable in its intensity that Pip buried him again as quickly as he could. (Compare Leo Colston's utter erasure of his memory of the terrible shadow of Marian's and Ted's love-making in L. P. Hartley's *The Go-Between* (1953); he speaks of the restoration of his memory when he achieves it fifty years later in terms of disinterment and exhumation, the bursting of 'cerements . . . coffins, . . . vaults' (Penguin edn (1975), Prologue.)) Now that Pip is three times older than he was then, the pressures of the contained memory have built up sufficiently to allow Magwitch to irrupt again, this time more permanently. If we should ask why Pip is 'three-and-twenty years of age' at the time of Magwitch's return, then one horrifyingly apposite answer might lie concealed, once more, in *A Tale of Two Cities*, where twenty-three is Sydney Carton's death number in the procession of those mounting to the guillotine:

The murmuring of many voices, the upturning of many faces, the pressing on of many footsteps in the outskirts of the crowd, so that it swells forward in a mass like one great heave of water, all flashes away. Twenty-Three. (III. 15)

The stormy rain that is one of the omens of Magwitch's return, anticipating the watery death-struggle in the Thames in chapter 54, picks up the apocalyptic water simile from this sentence describing Carton's last moment to suggest, in connection with 'Twenty-Three', that Magwitch is Death himself.

Magwitch, however ready Pip might be for his reappearance,

nevertheless still irrupts illegally from that recently discovered country 'from whose bourn' no transportee should return (*Hamlet*, III. i). He has come back by sea ('sea-tossed and sea-washed, months and months') on a journey which, accompanied as it is by Magwitch's expressed desire now 'to sleep long and sound', has overtones of *The Tempest*'s magical metamorphosis of the father's body (and memory) in 'Full fathom five thy father lies' ('Nothing of him that doth fade,/But doth suffer a sea-change'), as well as of the mystery enshrouded in ancient ship burials as tapped by Tennyson in *In Memoriam*, poems 8 and 10, the Lady of Shalott's death journey, and Arthur's voyage at the end of his *Morte d'Arthur*. The penalty for return, Magwitch claims, technically correctly (see above, p. 66), is death, which holds no fear for him because

'I'm a old bird now, as has dared all manner of traps ... and I'm not afeerd to perch upon a scarecrow. If there's Death hid inside of it, there is, and let him come out, and then I'll face him . . .' (chapter 40)

On the superficial narrative level he admits to having lived with the threat of death too long to care about it; the deeper drift of what he says is that he needs, like the Ghost of Old Hamlet, simply to be laid to rest, to be released from the agitating vault that is Pip's mind.

When, in order to disguise Magwitch, powder is applied to his head, Pip says:

But I can compare the effect of it, when on, to nothing but the probable effect of rouge upon the dead; so awful was the manner in which everything in him that it was most desirable to repress, started through that thin layer of pretence . . . (chapter 40)

The simile reveals the fact: he *is* dead (and therefore Death), and it is not possible to make a dead person look alive, to disguise his otherness from the world of living mortals. Magwitch, in other words, is the 'ghost of [Pip's] own father', to use Joe's phrase from chapter 27 again, finally having broken through the layers of repression that have kept him buried within the unplumbed recesses of Pip's memory for so many years. Now, finally, Pip re-enacts what Hamlet went through when the coughing phantom apprehended him at the beginning of that performance in chapter 31. 'I doubt if a ghost could have been more terrible to me', says Pip, driving the point home.

Another way of interpreting this manifestation of Magwitch,

known, identified, and scrutinized as he is by Pip and agreed by him to be dead, is to see him as a text to be read in the same way the gravestone is read by Pip in chapter 1 for the evidence it can offer as to the father's identity and deadness. If Magwitch can finally be 'read' as dead, then stage 3 consists, in effect, of the funeral preparations climaxing in the actual interment. To put it slightly differently, Magwitch's return this time enables Pip to undertake the procedures and rituals of burial which were denied him and which he has denied himself up until now. However, Pip's problem still seems to be that he can never finally relinquish his parents: Magwitch and Miss Havisham, like Mrs Joe, die slowly, and when dead they still haunt him (hence the return to the graveyard with little Pip in the final chapter).

On yet another level, the necrology of *Great Expectations* can be read as a cultural protest. In a period of graveyard reform and, more to the point, the reform of funeral epigraphy, Pip's refusal to pause and meditate the commonplaces of mortality by the graveside, and his insistence on opening the grave up, mark a negation of the contemporary urge to beautify, and thus erase, the fact of death and thereby the reality of the dead. To deny their selfhood, *Great Expectations* read in this way affirms, is to deny that they ever were. As a recent critic has remarked, the taming of tombstone epigraphy and the blandness of memorial iconography of the kind sported by Wemmick on his brooch (chapter 21) 'achieved the image of a beautiful death by repressing not only death and grief, but even the efforts to repress them, so that nothing is felt to lurk, and nothing threatens to return' (Karen Sánchez-Eppler, 'Decomposing: Wordsworth's Poetry of Epitaph and English Burial Reform', *Nineteenth-Century Literature*, 43 (1988), 415–31. On the larger questions raised here, see Philippe Ariès's *The Hour of Our Death*, tr. Helen Weaver (Penguin, 1983) and the same author's *Images of Man and Death*, tr. Janet Lloyd (Harvard University Press, 1985).) Pip's refusal to leave the dead alone can thus be read as not so much repellently materialistic as, rather, a refusal to conspire with contemporary pieties, an affirmation that the dead must not be allowed to disappear into the platitudes of lapidary formulae but must be constantly irritated into existence through the resurrective formulae of his own text. This is the case that *Hamlet* also presents us with, of course, and it is worth pondering; but we should ponder it in the light of Nietzsche's reminder that there has to be a 'boundary at which the past has to be forgotten if it is not to become the gravedigger of the present' ('The Use and Abuse of History', in *Untimely Meditations*, tr. R. J. Hollingdale (Cambridge: Cambridge University Press, 1983), p. 62).

At this stage though, (chapter 40), Pip still denies the full knowledge of the text that Magwitch threatens him with, and rushes off to Jaggers and the two casts and hence, with the interview of chapter 36 in his mind, the security of Jaggers's office as churchyard with its graves neatly closed, its tombstones there only to be sat upon. He needs to be told that this man is not his 'second father' (or, his father the second time round). But he is. Pip is Magwitch's son as Estella is his and Molly's daughter. He is of Magwitch's stock, and Magwitch is the stone come to deadly life.

From the fact of the return Dickens also develops parables deriving from Magwitch's ineluctable and ineradicable appearance as 'Prisoner, Felon, Bondsman', which is society's epitaph on him. Confronted now, again, with the father as prisoner, Pip's horror, greater here than it was at the beginning of the novel in some ways, is the horror of self-disgust, marker of his admission that Magwitch is the prisoner of his own grave-digging imagination, that he is a bondsman not just because society has made him so but because he is the product of Pip's necrophiliac obsessions, the *bound man* wrapped in his cerements. On another level, though, the recognition is simply humane: Pip's 'I knew him' (chapter 39) is a statement of kinship rooted in the human brother- and sisterhood rather than merely genetic affiliation, and Magwitch's tear-filled eyes mark his gratitude at being thus recognized as Abel rather than 'vagabond' Cain (Genesis 4:12). He has laboured like Adam; he has been a sheep-farmer like biblical Abel; now Pip curses him for 'risk[ing] his life to come to me [leaving] it in [his] keeping', his curse ghosting Cain's 'am I my brother's keeper', which chimes with the easterly wind that announced Magwitch's return (see stage I, section 2 above) to iterate the knowledge that tampering with the dead as Pip constantly does *is*, from one point of view at least, a Cainlike interference with their right to be left alone and therefore a symbolic murder, a second dismembering of them rather than a reflective re-membering of them.

And, as I have said, Pip is also Cainlike in his Oedipal hatred of Magwitch. If the Oedipal denial of the father is to be lifted, Pip's text explains, it will be done so only by anatomizing the nature of his kinship with the father. Magwitch starts off in chapter 39 as Pip's 'dreadful burden' (gigantic version of the burden he imposed in the form of the 'secret burden' down Pip's trouser leg in chapter 2) but ends up 'a gentle pressure' on Pip's hand (chapter 57).

The journey from chapter 39 to chapter 57 is, though, a long one. Magwitch's understandably aggressive requirement that Herbert swear on the 'little clasped black book' not to tell anyone anything about him echoes Old Hamlet's 'swear' in *Hamlet*, I. v, repeated as it is by Hamlet's own 'consent to swear . . . Never to speak of this that you have seen' to Horatio; and Magwitch's ghostly echo forces Pip to explore himself as the Magwitch-father's creation, as the deformed echo of a deformed echo, by explicitly introducing *Frankenstein* into his text. Pip's psychological probings are, however, shadowed by revelations of a more wide-ranging social nature. (It is worth recalling here, as Marjorie Garber has reminded us, that for Karl Marx the Ghost of Old Hamlet working away under the ground in I. v was an image of the subterranean growth of the Revolution: 'Empire will leap from its seat and exultantly exclaim, "Well grubbed, old mole!"' (Marx, *The Eighteenth Brumaire of Louis Bonaparte*, cit. Garber, *Shakespeare's Ghost Writers: Literature as Uncanny Causality* (New York and London: Methuen, 1987), p. 195). Pip is a gentleman because transported felon Magwitch made a lot of money down under as a sheep-farmer. This evolutionary move on Pip's part does not erase Magwitch but coexists with him, just as in biological evolution progressive and regressive forms live alongside each other. When Pip reverts to the chain image to say 'the wretched man, after loading wretched me with his gold and silver chains for years, had risked his life to come to me', he brilliantly focuses the mutuality of obligation. In defining and enchaining prisoners, society assumes responsibility for them; in accepting the gifts of money and becoming a gentleman by their means, Pip owes an obligation to Magwitch and is, in fact, his bondsman, just as he is his bondsman in being his son (as in Cordelia's 'I love your Majesty/According to my bond' to her father in *King Lear*, I. i).

Later a further, and fundamentally humanist as well as Christian, perception dawns on Pip: that even if he refuses to accept any more money, the obligation still remains. It is at this point, of course, that the symbolic value of the father-son theme becomes fully apparent. For parental-filial links are the closest ones human beings know, which is why they supply Judaism, Christianity and other religions, with their traditional paternal/maternal iconography. And that is why Dickens locates them at the base of his parable of interdependence in *Great Expectations*.

Chapters 39 and 40 record Pip's horror at Magwitch's return, then, even referring to the uncanny power of Magwitch's 'wicked spirit' at the end of chapter 39, which turns him into Pip's cacodaemon; and this reaction remains primary at the opening of stage 3. At the same time, though, Magwitch is permitted to tell his own story; so that the beginning of stage 3 also admits into the narrative an alternative voice to Pip's own, the voice of the parental other which, whatever the similarities between its history and that of its son (Pip's), nevertheless insists on the individuality of its own existence, insists that its 'I' is not Pip's 'I', and that it is not, in fact, Pip's property to be exhumed at will like the skeleton in the church in chapter 8. In effect, Magwitch's voice undermines Pip's, and Herbert's too (as the 'old mole' in *Hamlet*, I. v literally undermines that other pair, Hamlet and Horatio), and Pip, like Hamlet, is forced, before coming to terms with him, to recast him as uncle: 'I do not even know ... by what name to call you. I have given out that you are my uncle' (chapter 40). Which makes him Pip's version of Claudius, the father-as-enemy, undermining Provis the provider by identifying him with the villainous poisoner of Denmark's ear, the narrator of false and venomous histories. This is one way Pip tries to disparage the validity of Magwitch's words. And before Magwitch is allowed to open 'the book of his remembrance' (chapter 42) to us, to create himself through his autobiography, Pip attempts to disparage him further by associating him with *Frankenstein*.

Stage 3 CHAPTERS 40–59

1. *Frankenstein* and the Zombie *chapter 40*

Thematically, stage 3 is characterized by its recapitulation of the symbols and signs released in the previous two stages, though in purely narrative terms it achieves a pace and excitement that matches those of stage 1, the question now being not so much 'who is Pip's benefactor?' as 'who is the mysterious stranger shadowing Magwitch in the darkness at the beginning of chapter 40, and is he the same person as the one who, according to the Watchman, was "with" Magwitch when he arrived the previous night?' The answer – that they are two different people whom we know of already and who now become inextricably entwined as each other's double, namely Orlick and Compeyson – emerges only slowly; though it is important to note here that Compeyson, an obscure figure in stage 1, and scarcely thought of at all in stage 2, now becomes a – if not the – central figure. It is not only that he is the man who betrayed Miss Havisham (chapter 42) but that he possesses this extraordinary twinship with Magwitch as Orlick and Drummle do with Pip. Stage 3, then, might well be entitled 'the struggle of the doubles' as it recalls that image, released so dramatically in stage 1, of Magwitch wrestling with Compeyson in the ditch (a moment recalled verbatim by Pip in chapter 39) and revives Orlick in all his malevolence.

Simultaneously, though, Compeyson's link with Miss Havisham connects with the world of Pip's mothers. In emphasizing the world of the fathers in stage 3, Pip does not overlook this crucial aspect of his own Oedipal psychology. Magwitch appeared in the narrative prior to Miss Havisham, and she dies before him, so that her story is contained within his larger one as women's history has, by and large, been ingested by patriarchal history. This textual fact proves that Pip's primary concern is with the father-as-obstacle, though it does not diminish the power of the Miss Havisham story and its mystery. Indeed, by framing it and thereby rendering it central, it increases its significance. Interesting confirmation of this comes, I think, from Pip's introduction of *Frankenstein* at the beginning of stage 3, as he tries to understand his relationship with his father by exploring the implications of an image generated by a text written by a woman.

The influence of Mary Shelley's *Frankenstein; or the Modern*

Prometheus (1818) was considerable in the nineteenth century, and its role in *Great Expectations* is more far-reaching than the one overt reference to it might seem to suggest. The reference comes at the end of chapter 40:

> When he was not asleep, or playing a complicated kind of Patience with a ragged pack of cards of his own – a game that I never saw before or since, and in which he recorded his winnings by sticking his jack-knife into the table – when he was not engaged in either of these pursuits, he would ask me to read to him – 'Foreign language, dear boy!' While I complied, he, not comprehending a single word, would stand before the fire surveying me with the air of an Exhibitor, and I would see him, between the fingers of the hand with which I shaded my face, appealing in dumb show to the furniture to take notice of my proficiency. The imaginary student pursued by the misshapen creature he had impiously made, was not more wretched than I, pursued by the creature who had made me . . .

We have met the idea of the Exhibitor before in Wemmick's 'would you like to have a look at Newgate?' (chapter 32), and the dirty and drunk minister of justice who offers Pip 'a full view of the Lord Chief Justice [as if he were] a waxwork'. (These remind us not only of the Victorian commitment to shows and spectacle but of the Victorian fascination with the deprived, the deranged and the dead.) The Exhibitors in this novel, then, are in a sense doubles for Pip the narrator, inviting us to admit that we are being seduced by Pip into peeping into a charnel and into watching zombies perform at his will as he summons them from the depths of his unconscious. But the juxtaposition of Exhibitor here against the Frankenstein myth demonstrates the extent to which Pip the creator of his characters is, like Frankenstein, himself the victim of his creatures. Magwitch, a zombie in the literal sense of one returned from the dead and reanimated, performs the role of Exhibitor of Pip, whom he bids perform a mechanical and meaningless task for his gratification, thereby turning Pip himself metaphorically into a zombie, the manifest creation of his own deadness. (Note how, afterwards, he compels Pip to become housebound – in effect, gravebound – except when, by night, he accompanies his father-creator as an unwilling shadow: 'I dared not go out, except when I took Provis for an airing after dark' (end of chapter 40).)

The general relevance of *Frankenstein* to *Great Expectations* is clear: Frankenstein creates his creature, runs away from it in horror at its ugliness, its apparent unfittedness for survival in the world as it is, and is vengefully pursued by it. Disowned by its creator it systematically destroys everyone whom its creator loves. Described this simply, the story puts a dark perspective on Magwitch's creation of Pip into a gentleman and makes Pip's awareness of his future as a gentleman deeply ironical, registering his social bastardy, his status as an outcast. It casts an equally black shadow on Miss Havisham's relationship with Estella. In adopting and forming her she has abused the role of mother and become a Frankenstein too, producing a creature who, because she was unloved, is incapable of love and is, like the creature, a form of avenger. But, as in *Frankenstein*, the problem is in part an aetiological one, leading us right back through the parental chain. If Estella is the creature to Miss Havisham's creator, then Miss Havisham herself, as the novel's arch-revenger, is the product of the pain of absolute rejection. *Her* Frankenstein is Compeyson, the gentleman forger, the false creator, the creator of falsehood. And who forged the forger to be as he is?

Yet the simile at the end of chapter 40 actually offers an analogy between Pip and Frankenstein and Magwitch and 'the misshapen creature', thereby inviting a reading of Pip's relationship with Magwitch that supports the rather sinister emphasis I have placed on it in this study. If Pip is the 'student' and Magwitch 'the misshapen creature' then Pip in the graveyard of chapter 1 and in the crypt of his autobiographical text (to use the Derridean notion of language's incapacity to prevent stable meaning from succumbing to the process of decomposition) has created Magwitch. (See Jacques Derrida, 'Fors', tr. Barbara Johnson, *The Georgia Review*, vol. 31 (1977), pp. 64–116.) He has, however, created him in a rather specific way, as dreams mentioned early on in chapter 2, and now returning even more terribly with Magwitch, compel us to acknowledge ('my rest broken by fearful dreams', chapter 40). For Pip's dreams are not so much the bad dreams of *Hamlet*, II. ii ('I could be bounded in a nutshell and count myself king of infinite space – were it not that I have bad dreams') as they are Frankenstein's nightmare appropriation of his dead mother's body at the moment of his creature's completion:

I slept, indeed, but I was disturbed by the wildest dreams. I thought I saw Elizabeth, in the bloom of health, walking in the streets of Ingolstadt. Delighted and surprised, I embraced her; but as I imprinted the first kiss on her lips, they became livid with the hue of death; her features appeared to change, and I thought that I beheld the corpse of my dead mother in my arms; a shroud enveloped her form, and I saw the grave-worms crawling in the folds of the flannel. I started from my sleep with horror . . . (*Frankenstein*, ed. Maurice Hindle (Penguin, 1985), chapter 5)

He kisses his adopted sister Elizabeth, who decomposes into the corpse of his dead mother. Frankenstein then awakens into a world which is haunted by the presence of his creature. If we recall that the creature is formed from the corpse fragments gathered from charnels, then we realize, with a sense of shock, that Dickens is actually using the *Frankenstein* allusion here to tell us something about Pip's – and even his own – imaginative powers: that Magwitch in chapter 1, as on his return in chapter 39, is the creature of Pip's fancy, a ghost imagined into being by him out of the remains of his dead father lying beneath the ground in his coffin; and that Miss Havisham bears the same relationship to his dead mother.

We have, of course, known or suspected this all along. Being told in this way, however, makes us realize even more fully the extent to which Pip, as the caller-into-being of his dead parents, is responsible for them. If you summon the dead and they come to you in dreams or as ghosts (or as Frankenstein's creature) you cannot simply disown them, or shrug them off. To deny them is to risk perpetual haunting until their needs are met. Deny them and you become Cain, or an interminably delaying Hamlet.

Both Magwitch and Miss Havisham, therefore, are reassembled (or re-membered) by Pip, by analogy with Frankenstein, from the corpses of his dead parents, and the story of Pip's relationship with them is the narrative of his coming-to-terms with himself in relation to them. But the final direct clue to emerge from the *Frankenstein* passage is this: that if in his dream Frankenstein reaches the image of his dead mother through visualizing his adopted sister, then in the 'fearful dream' that is *Great Expectations*, Estella is Pip's sister through the Magwitch connection; she is his route to the body of his dead mother in the shape of shrouded Miss Havisham. That is why she is his guide to her from the beginning; that is why he fuses (or confuses) the two as he does at the end of chapter 8. *Frankenstein*, in fact, is one of our major clues to the psychology of the uncanny as it presents itself in *Great Expectations*.

In this connection, it is no accident that the chapter which ends with *Frankenstein* begins:

The impossibility of keeping him concealed in the chambers was self-evident. It could not be done, and the attempt to do it would inevitably engender suspicion. True, I had no Avenger in my service now, but I was looked after by an inflammatory old female, assisted by an animated rag-bag whom she called her niece . . .

We have not been told before of the disappearance of Pepper, the Avenger, presumably because he and the two women are present in the narrative at all only as the products of Pip's psychological situation. The woman and her niece – now that Magwitch has burst the boundaries of the grave, terrible in his powder 'like rouge upon the dead' – are doubles of Miss Havisham and Estella, completing for Pip as he surveys Magwitch in his full horror his imagined family in a kind of dumb show. 'Animated rag-bag' strikingly reinforces the zombie-suggestiveness of this area of the novel; and a page later Pip, 'in a sort of dream or sleep-waking', finds it difficult to distinguish her head 'from her dusty broom', again, presumably because she is one of the dusty dead who has been called back to animated half-life. Pip, like Frankenstein, in his dreaming and his waking life, creates and recreates the dead.

Yet, to move beyond *Frankenstein* now, if a crude translation of the image of the old lady and her niece is that they 'represent' Miss Havisham and Estella, a subtler reading might be that the niece herself denotes Miss Havisham in her ragged dress and that the two therefore restate Pip's obsession with Estella as a phase of Miss Havisham (we recall how when Pip first saw her he apprehended her as both girl and old woman simultaneously). The effect of this becomes even more surreal when we link the girl's (and Miss Havisham's) raggedness with the 'ragged pack of cards' with which Magwitch plays Patience, recording his score with his jack-knife. For here, too, we are in the world of psychological symbol – Pip's heightened hallucinatory state that is at once the cause and result of Magwitch's return. The *jack*-knife catches up all the other jacks that we have encountered in the novel, reminding us that in the end *jack* signifies that simple Adamic 'jack self' that knew that Knaves were Jacks (until told otherwise) and then fabricated Jaggers as an accusatory guilt-inducing reminder of this jack self once his social standing had changed. It evokes Pip's basic earthy self in another way, too: *jack* is a further sign of the connections between *Great Expectations* and *A Tale of Two Cities* in recalling for us that Defarge's revolutionary henchmen in that novel are known as *Jacques*: Jacques One, Jacques Two, Jacques Three ... Magwitch's card game revives the jacks also, of course, by reliving the game first played by Pip and Estella while Miss Havisham looked on 'corpse-like', and the game played at Satis in chapter 29 at which Jaggers is a dominating 'cold presence' and which, as it tells of loss of fortune and the abasing of 'Kings and Queens', becomes, like Beggar My Neighbour in chapter 8, an emblem of Pip's own rise and decline, of his gain and loss of the self created by Magwitch.

2. Magwitch's Story *chapter 42*

Before Magwitch tells his story to Pip and 'Pip's comrade' (chapter 42) he makes Herbert swear secrecy on his 'greasy little clasped black Testament' (chapter 39), thereby reinforcing his affinity with the Ghost of Old Hamlet with his 'swear' in *Hamlet*, I. v. His story itself is rather different from Old Hamlet, though, in being one of deprivation and crime, and it is completed in chapters 50 and 51. Its main substance is presented in chapter 42, however, as Magwitch narrates a brief autobiography that, as a fictional device, has its origins in the inset autobiographies of eighteenth-century picaresque romance (Mr Wilson's in Book 3 of Fielding's *Joseph Andrews*, for instance, and those of the Man of the Hill and Mrs Fitzpatrick in Books 8 and 11 of *Tom Jones* respectively). Such narratives are often designed to parallel the life story of the hero/heroine of the novel in which they are presented, in part to offer moral exempla in the form of warning or encouragement to imitation, but more importantly to demonstrate kinship. Wilson's history doubles Joseph's life story because *Joseph Andrews* is about its hero's search for his lost father as much as it is about his quest for Fanny; and the Man of the Hill reflects Tom's life back at him because Tom, too, is an orphan in search of a father. Dickens, whose enjoyment of Fielding was so considerable that he named one of his sons Henry Fielding Dickens after him, is thus writing in a tradition of confessional inset narratives as they are used in fictions embodying a patriarchal quest. The fact that Frankenstein's creature is given a long inset tale in which he recounts to his creator his whole experience of his wakening into being is also relevant, as is the fact that Mary Shelley's direct model here was the 'wakening into being' narratives of Adam and Eve in Milton's *Paradise Lost*. In *Frankenstein*, however, the creature accuses his creator for denying him love and the liberties that should be enjoyed by any living creature: myth (Prometheus tormented by Zeus's eagle, Satan outcast by God in Milton's version of their primal antagonism for daring not to acknowledge God's parenthood) carries here the message of political freedom in a way characteristic of romantic fables. And it does so in *Great Expectations*, too, as Magwitch repeats for the second time, in the same words that he used in chapter 40, that he is 'Magwitch, chrisen'd Abel'.

It is a formula that turns this marginal and 'ragged little creetur' whose life he sums up as 'in jail and out of jail, in jail and out of jail' into a symbolic son of Adam and Eve, imaging the rootlessness and ultimate loneliness of all of us. The way he describes being 'locked up, as much as a silver tea-kettle' renders the process of jailing a symptom of society's commodity fetishism, its hoarding care of the criminal as object; so that one of the things Magwitch's tale focuses on is the paternalism at the heart of the prison system as it had developed since the end of the eighteenth century. Over Magwitch's rootlessness, in other words, hangs a question mark interrogating the nature of paternalism in all its forms as, over Pip, there hangs a noose querying the nature of the dead father.

Magwitch (the name becomes no less riddling for its repetition: he has some elemental magical quality to be popping up here, there, and everywhere, but we can't pin it down any more than that), 'chrisen'd Abel', is all our dead brothers back to the beginning of time whose deaths are accusations against the God who created them mortal and suffering and who are crying out for vengeance and succour and remembrance. As he tells Pip in a revelation that is startling because it applies to more of us than we may at first realize: 'I've no more notion where I was born, than you have'. Simultaneously, knowing – just knowing, without (apparently) the benefit of formal instruction that 'the birds' names in the hedges [were] chaffinch, sparrer, thrush' – makes him Adamic in this novel of postlapsarian landscapes, reminding us that Adam named the creatures as a sign of a lordship over the earth that in Magwitch's case is sadly lacking. If Adam was at once mud and spirit, then Magwitch is mud with the spirit taken out of him and with lordship denied in consequence. Like so many other people and things in this novel, he is merely 'ragged' – like the ragged niece, like Miss Havisham gradually dissolving into dust with her clothes, like Magwitch's entropic pack of cards, all of which remind us that kings and queens as well as 'Golden lads and girls all must/As chimney sweepers, come to dust' (Shakespeare's *Cymbeline*, IV. ii).

Magwitch's story is in many ways the novel's omphalos, its link with the body of society that also proclaims disjunction and severance, a testament to the fact of orphanhood and deprivation in a country and a world to which religion, the idea of a saving beneficent deity, can offer consolation only to those who, in the material sense, are the possessors and thus the inheritors of the earth. Christianity, the novel suggests, comforts the comfortable;

and those who are comfortable neglect the little children who are at the centre of one of Christ's most important messages. Therefore this 'little creetur' that was the young Magwitch is known to be *hardened*, reflecting in the injustice of that word Fagin's boy criminals, Jo the crossing sweeper of *Bleak House* and, since certain well-intentioned middle-class Christian men and women 'giv me tracts what I couldn't read', Pip himself when bound apprentice and assailed by a tract in chapter 13.

Magwitch's mention of hardening opens our eyes further to the implications of the word. We know Pip's mind. We have trusted him as he has told us how he developed. We know as he knows, because he keeps on telling us, how hardened (unkind) he has been towards Joe. Magwitch's use of the word suggests a root cause: hardening, externally or internally induced, has its origin in loss of love, loss of openness to others. As Pip becomes more a member of society, and adult, as that concept is understood in romantic psychology, he loses the capacity for love and openness because society demands that you suppress your feelings, that you bury your core, childhood, self (see Dirk den Hartog, *Dickens and Romantic Psychology* (London and Basingstoke: Macmillan, 1987), chapter 1 and *passim*). This in turn means that behaviour in society will tend to secrecy, to the operation of closed systems, suppression. Secrecy is the condition of buried feelings. Openness is the equivalent of dream-work, the summoning of suppressed feelings to the light of day. And this leads Pip and us to Estella, whose stock (in the sense of originator) Magwitch is, the girl brought up to be hardened, taught not to love as an emblem of Miss Havisham's buried wound, and, by a strange circle of coincidence, therefore the true daughter of her father after all.

At this point Magwitch introduces Compeyson, the most remote yet far-reaching shadow in the novel. We have seen him before, right at the beginning; we have learned a little bit more about him from Herbert in the third chapter of stage 2; we now find out, in the third chapter of stage 3, who he is. With 'no more heart than a iron file' – which locates his centre at the centre of the novel's symbolic code – he is 'as cold as death, and [has] the head of the Devil'.

Compeyson is root evil. Like Satan, he goes around 'seeking whom he may devour' (I Peter 5:8), and like him he is the arch-master of disguise, the master forger. His evil stains and touches upon everyone in the novel: Miss Havisham, her half-brother, Magwitch, Pip, Orlick, even Wopsle, who sees him as a chilling ghost at the performance of the play in chapter 47, and Herbert, into whose history, via Miss Havisham, Estella and Satis, he has also written himself. In placing this horrifying unknown at the base of the novel's plot Dickens invests him with appalling psychological and spiritual reality. He *is* all that any of the characters in the novel know of evil, the cause of death in life. This is how he could get Magwitch, street-wise though he is, 'into such nets as made me his black slave', with its half echo of the 'snare of the devil' (I Timothy 3:7) as well as of Pip's childhood 'meshes', the marshes from which Pip, like Magwitch, never escapes, be it in Satis's garden, Barnard's Inn, or on the lower reaches of the Thames near the end, which are 'like my own marsh country' (chapter 54).

But the fact that Pip is a gentleman as the result of his kindness to Magwitch on those marshes is now, because of Compeyson's slippery gentility, open to radical reinterpretation. Magwitch, it appears from chapter 42, created Pip a gentleman in order to match, to correspond to, Compeyson. He engineered him to avenge himself on the man who, at the trial which he tells us about in this chapter, showed up so much the better for having been to public school. This is one of the most pointed accusations that Dickens aims at the processes of the judicial system and the society it is designed to protect; for to be affected by appearances and to be taken in by them is (if the metaphor is followed through to its origins in the nakedness and clothing of Genesis 3) to prove oneself a victim of the Fall, a son of Satan. A gentleman in the vocabulary of this novel is a gentle man in the particular form of Joe, Compeyson's exact opposite, showing kindness to the 'poor miserable fellow-creatur' Magwitch at the end of chapter 5. Dickens has created a sign system in *Great Expectations* which identifies those who are not gentle men with the devil. That, we now see, is why Drummle is a brute of almost allegorical proportions and a double of Orlick, whose name *now* sounds a bit like 'Old Nick'; and that is why both are doubles of Pip, who approaches the nearer to them the further he moves from Joe.

The struggle between Compeyson and Magwitch at the beginning, as at the end, matched as it is by Pip's struggle on 'the brink of [his] grave' with Orlick in chapter 53, can also now be seen for what it ultimately is: a fight to the death with the devil. If Magwitch can vanquish Compeyson-Satan he will have overcome the forces in society that conspired to harden him in the first place. The forming of Pip into gentleman thus reads less like vicarious emulation of

Compeyson than it does as erasure and replacement of him and all he represents. If Pip *was* kind to Magwitch at the beginning then, Magwitch assumes, Pip the gentleman will be kind, too. Magwitch's shock on his return to discover Pip's disgust at him – to discover Pip as Compeyson – is itself almost too horrifying to contemplate.

At the heart of Magwitch's tale, though, as we have seen, lie Compeyson, Miss Havisham and Arthur, and hence another restatement of Pip's kinship problems; for Compeyson, betrothed to Miss Havisham, 'is' Pip's father. (If we doubt this we have only to note Magwitch's comment about Compeyson's 'curly hair and . . . black clothes' (chapter 42) and compare Pip's fantasy over the paternal gravestone at the beginning that his father had 'curly black hair'.) The images of the fathers proliferate in this novel, as do those of the mothers, because Pip's narrative and its inset narratives obsessively relive the primal loss and its consequences in the form of alienation, displacement, guilt and so forth.

This makes Arthur particularly interesting. On one level, he is another symptom of the widespread Victorian interest in forms of insanity or hallucinatory disease, a companion for Miss Havisham seen as a clinical case history. On another level, though, he is yet another, and extreme, image of Pip. Dying with 'the horrors on him' (*delirium tremens*), he has an hallucination of Miss Havisham as a mad woman (that is, as both insane and angry), her heart broken and bleeding, holding a shroud out to him. It is as if Pip, receiving this picture via Magwitch, is viewing himself seeing Miss Havisham in the form of a disturbed ecstatic dream. For Pip is, after all, the one who imagined this corpselike woman into existence in the first place; it is only Pip, and now Arthur, whose word we have for it that 'she's all in white . . . wi' white flowers in her hair, and she's awful mad'. And when Arthur dies, screaming, 'Here she is! She's got the shroud again. She's unfolding it. She's coming out of the corner', we realize that Magwitch as the returned dead father is disclosing to Pip through Arthur's death a perception about his 'son's' commitment to the mother. Arthur dying, however unwillingly, into Miss Havisham re-enacts an essential – *the* essential – wish-fulfilment for Pip, the underlying purpose of whose life is to die into his dead mother, earthbound Georgiana. It is, of course, a disclosure of the Oedipal secret in yet another form; one that is not unlike Freud's later description of the mother as Death in his essay 'The Theme of the Three Caskets'. (It is here that Freud writes about mythological and other groupings of three women, relating them to the triad of the Fates who, in ancient classical thought, spun, wove and cut the thread of life, and identifying them with the three women in a man's life: 'the mother herself, the beloved one who is chosen after her pattern, and lastly the Mother Earth who receives him once more. But it is in vain that the old man yearns for the love of woman, as he had it first from his mother; the third of the Fates alone, the silent Goddess of Death, will take him into her arms' (*Standard Edition of the Complete Psychological Works of Sigmund Freud*, ed. James Strachey et al., vol. 12, p. 301).) Pip's subsequent struggle with Miss Havisham in chapter 49, fired, as it were, by Magwitch's account of Arthur's death, is a re-vision of that death, an attempt to deny the mother-as-Death (and to deny that she is dead) by trying to save her life, which succeeds in turning them into 'desperate enemies' as Pip struggles, apparently, to kill her, to commit her finally to the grave.

3. The End of Miss Havisham *chapters 43–44, 49*

Pip visits Miss Havisham twice in stage 3, in chapters 43–4 and chapter 49. He hears of her death from Joe in chapter 57. The first visit involves Estella; the second concerns the financial arrangements Pip is making for Herbert's partnership in Clarriker's.

The landscape of Pip's home country as described in chapter 43 – and, indeed, the whole visit – develops out of Magwitch's life story as recounted in the preceding chapter, for when 'day [comes] creeping on, halting and whimpering and shivering, and wrapped in patches of clouds and rags of mist like a beggar', it is as if it and the countryside it illuminates are a redefinition of the beggarly Magwitch of the autobiography and a ghostly evocation of the 'bundle of shivers' that is Pip at the beginning. In other words, this dawn and this visit take us back to the past; so that when Drummle appears, 'toothpick in hand', we know, as we never did before, that he is, as Estella's suitor, a manifestation in the present of the brutish gentleman Compeyson wooing Miss Havisham all those years earlier. Drummle's momentary juxtaposition against a man who looks like Orlick at the end of the chapter confirms the identification, for Orlick is now employed by Compeyson.

The short chapter (44) in which Pip now confronts Miss Havisham and Estella – over his frustrated hopes, over Drummle, over the possibility of helping Herbert – reinforces the time-warp aspect as Estella occupies herself throughout the interview by knitting. As Pip addresses Miss Havisham, Estella's knitting reminds us of the three Fates and the tricoteuses in *A Tale of Two Cities* as Sydney Carton goes to the guillotine, and therefore, again, of death; while the rows of the knitting as they grow duplicate the chains of obligation and dependence that bind the characters to each other in the novel either umbilically or, as in the case of Magwitch's 'nets' in chapter 42, through another form of compulsion. More specifically, in view of what we discover about Molly in chapter 48, they also suggest the link, through matriliny, between her and Estella. For as a prelude to the return to Miss Havisham in chapter 49, Pip visits Jaggers, sees Molly again, and hears Molly's story from Wemmick. A nervous action of Molly's fingers 'was like the action of knitting' and Pip makes the 'link': 'I felt absolutely certain that this woman was

Estella's mother'. Molly the avenger who gave away her child in revenge against Magwitch, now the tamed mad woman, is here finally not just 'bound' to her daughter but brought into alignment with mad Miss Havisham, too, as the arch-mother behind the novel's plot. Molly, 'really' Estella's mother, identified and placed in Pip's memory as an image, enables Pip to say farewell to that other powerful maternal image, Miss Havisham.

In many ways chapter 49 is a formal elegy, recapturing the tone used earlier of the Richmond house:

> The cathedral chimes had at once a sadder and a more remote sound to me ... than they had ever had before; so, the swell of the old organ was borne to my ears like funeral music; and the rooks, as they hovered about the grey tower and swung in the bare high trees of the priory-garden, seemed to call to me that the place was changed, and that Estella was gone out of it for ever.

But it is clear that the loss of Estella metaphorically substitutes for the loss of the mother who is now, at last, after Pip's long and agonized resurrection of her, to be laid to rest. Hence youthful Estella is replaced as the guardian of the threshold to Miss Havisham by 'an elderly woman whom [Pip] had never seen before', image of Death herself. And Miss Havisham is even more faded, remote and lonely, seated 'in a ragged chair' and contemplating an ashy fire. The details suggest that the memory of her is being relinquished by Pip, that he is relegating her finally to the solitude of the grave where she can now lie undisturbed. The fact that she agrees to give Pip the £900 on Herbert's behalf is significant in this respect because she does it to 'show [Pip] that I am not all stone'. For this takes us right back to chapter 1 and the mother under the tombstone and to Pip's tendency to identify maternal deadness with stony hard-heartedness.

Pip, who has always generated hostile, prickly, cold-hearted mothers (Mrs Joe, Miss Havisham, Molly in a way), has constantly been on the attack, repudiating the feminine because he felt it repudiated him. His invention of a stone-hearted Miss Havisham and the further invention of stone-hearted Estella made Georgiana's tombstone real. Pip can release his mother of stone when she can be proved to be loving.

When she gives the money Miss Havisham shows signs of being 'not all stone'; when she turns to Pip, perceives the full extent of his grief over Estella, kneels, weeps ('I had never seen her shed a tear before'), and calls Pip 'my Dear', revealing 'an earnest womanly compassion', she becomes the loving mother he always sought. But what he says about her mind having grown diseased in her dark solitude is, in fact, true as a description of his own long and morbid period of grief for his dead parents; and her tale of how she turned to stone is 'really' the story of how Pip, in his mourning, invented for himself a family of stone figures to match those in the graves in the churchyard. As he walks away, retracing his memories through his footsteps (they are among the most significant ones in his autobiography: the corner where he fought Herbert; the path where he and Estella walked together), he imagines Miss Havisham dead again, 'hanging to the beam'.

Pip had always known his mother was dead even while he fantasized her back to life, but he had opposed that fancy with the stronger one that she was, nevertheless, somehow actually alive. Now that he can lay her to rest he still, as we have seen, rejects the idea of her death. As he discovers her covered in flames he struggles with her like her 'desperate enemy', as if trying to sustain her in the role she has played in his imagination ever since he was a little boy way back in chapter 8.

4. The End of Magwitch *chapters 46–47, 52–56*

In order to effect Magwitch's escape, Pip and Herbert arrange for him to lodge in rooms above those inhabited by Clara's father, Bill Barley (chapter 46), thus literally realizing Pip's earliest image of his father as 'above' (chapter 1; opening of chapter 7) and of Magwitch as hanged, for he now seems to fuse with 'Old Barley growling in the beam' (chapter 46). The image of the hanged man who is 'above' is recalled because Pip is about to lay Magwitch to rest, too. Not surprisingly, therefore, the topography of Pip's walk to Chinks's Basin where he is to take up residence echoes that of his marshland home with its Hulks and its hulk of an Orlick. It is also reminiscent of Satis's garden:

> It matters not what stranded ships repairing in dry docks I lost myself among, what old hulls of ships in course of being knocked to pieces, what ooze and slime and other dregs of tide, what yards of ship-builders and ship-breakers, what rusty anchors blindly biting into the ground though for years off duty, what mountainous country of accumulated casks and timber, how many rope-walks that were not the Old Green Copper . . .

If Bill Barley – still heard but never seen, his death eagerly awaited – lacks any kind of reality as a character or even as a name, then that is because he is a phantom of the resurrected Magwitch, one created by Pip as a consolatory anticipation, a comic celebration, of paternal death, to enable him the more easily to part with Magwitch when the time comes (it is in this chapter that his role as hoarder of all the *provisions* chimes, on the same page, with the name *Provis*).

Another way Pip accommodates the difficulty of relinquishing Magwitch is to take refuge in the relief of a farcical play and its accompanying pantomime (chapter 47), the last of the novel's theatrical insets. He goes to the theatre after one of his practice rowing trips down the river whose ebbing tide will symbolize Magwitch's ebbing life to see Wopsle featuring in both entertainments; in both, symbols and motifs from the main text are exuberantly transformed as a reminder that in the world of the comic imagination resolutions can be offered and pain soothed away.

The play offers a fantasy on the whole of *Great Expectations* and a light-hearted rebuttal of the darkness of *Barnwell* and *Hamlet*, with its 'virtuous boatswain' with 'a bag of money in his pocket' who marries amid great rejoicing on Portsmouth beach but is then opposed by 'a certain dark-complexioned Swab ... whose heart was openly stated (by the boatswain) to be as black as his figure-head'. With Portsmouth as our clue – for it is the place where Magwitch made his landing, as he tells us in chapter 39 – it is not difficult to see Magwitch in the bosun loaded with money bags and Compeyson in the devilish opponent who proposes 'to two other Swabs to get all mankind into difficulties' (*swab* as a contemporary slang word for a naval officer's epaulette and a contemptuous term for an officer neatly implicates Compeyson the gentleman as well). The *deus ex machina* is Wopsle wearing star and garter who resolves all problems by placing the swabs in prison and giving the bosun 'a Union Jack as a slight acknowledgement of his public services'. *Jack* riddles quietly away here, embracing all the other Jacks in the novel, and somehow focusing the arch-Jack Jaggers, with his Britannia metal spoons (chapter 25) and his mastery of Little Britain.

The festive note, so at odds with Pip's black thoughts about Magwitch and Estella and the bleakness of the February night outside the theatre, continues in the second piece, a 'new grand comic Christmas pantomime' (Magwitch was captured on Christmas day at the beginning of the novel). Wopsle is seen first as an apprentice 'engaged in the manufacture of thunderbolts in a mine, and displaying great cowardice when his gigantic master came home', then as an enchanter who 'comes up from the antipodes rather unsteadily, after an apparently violent journey ... with a necromantic work in one volume under his arm' in response to a summons from the Genius of Youthful Love who is having a hard time 'on account of the parental brutality of an ignorant farmer who opposed the choice of his daughter's heart'.

It is not hard to see here a reflection of Pip at the forge and a zany transformation of Joe into the terrifying master from whom he has to escape, together with a metamorphosis of Magwitch into a genuine magician this time, just back from Australia in order to solve all Pip's problems in relation to Estella while dances, songs, and fireworks are aimed at him in celebration.

Nevertheless, the dark world suddenly impinges as Wopsle stares then glares at Pip and then, confused and in a kind of dream, recalls to Pip as they walk away afterwards that 'certain Christmas Day, when you were quite a child' when they caught the two convicts fighting, and proceeds to relieve himself of his burden of uncanny experience by revealing to Pip that Compeyson was sitting behind him in the audience. Pip comments:

> I cannot exaggerate the enhanced disquiet into which this conversation threw me, or the special and peculiar terror I felt at Compeyson's having been behind me 'like a ghost.' For, if he had ever been out of my thoughts for a few moments together since the hiding had begun, it was in those very moments when he was closest to me . . .

This is what one says of the devil, and Compeyson is, of course, black, like the swab (Magwitch describes him as 'dressed in black' at the trial in chapter 42). 'Like a ghost' is Wopsle's phrase, appropriated by Pip, to remind us that the world of pantomime festivity has now been displaced by the *Hamlet* world of paternal phantoms and that black Compeyson, that darkest of shadows, is as much an image of his father to Pip as Murdstone is to David in *David Copperfield*. All of which plunges Pip straight back into his world of bad dreams, stretched as his mind is between the territory of Wemmick's castle with its Aged P. safe, or apparently safe, and insulated from threats of parricide and ghosts, and the space that is Jaggers, whom Pip visits in chapter 48 only to find himself haunted by the memory of his night at the Hummums in chapter 45: 'the street lamp-lighters . . . were . . . opening up more red eyes in the gathering fog than my rushlight tower at the Hummums had opened white eyes in the ghostly wall'. (The light he mentions had looked 'like the ghost of a walking-cane'.) Then, in the office, a note of the ghostly uncanny sounds again: 'the pair of coarse fat office candles that dimly lighted Mr Jaggers as he wrote in a corner, were decorated with dirty winding sheets, as if in remembrance of a host of hanged clients'; for they parody 'the two casts on the shelf' who, illuminated by flames from the fire, 'look[ed] as if they were playing a diabolical game at bo-peep with me'.

The narrative returns to Magwitch in chapter 52 after another meeting with Jaggers and after Miss Havisham's accident. The meeting with Jaggers (chapter 51) is a crucial prelude to encountering Magwitch again, for it is here that Pip reveals to him the identity of Estella's father – the one thing that Jaggers, that arch-possessor of secrets, does not know. Yet when we hear Jaggers assure Pip 'he did not know who her father was', then talk about Estella's adoption, and then ask: 'For whose sake would you reveal the secret? For the father's? . . . For the mother's? . . . For the daughter's?', we sense that he is offering a valid comment on Pip's own history. Pip's pursuit of Estella's parents ('What purpose I had in view when I was hot on tracing out and proving Estella's parentage, I cannot say') is zealous because through it he is reworking the quest he started in chapter 1. And Jaggers's recommendation of secrecy after he knows the answer to the riddle is a possibility he offers to Pip: bury the dead; let them be. It is comically underlined by Pip's revelation to Jaggers of Wemmick's private life: ' "What's all this?" said Mr Jaggers. "You with an old father, and you with pleasant and playful ways?" ' Wemmick's schizoid split is, from the perspective of *this* chapter, perhaps not so pernicious after all. It is, rather, a way of assuring the necessary integrity of the private world.

The Wemmick twins remind us that it was Magwitch who brought Compeyson with him way back at the novel's beginning, raising him as a phantom evil father (they are dressed almost identically in their respective boats in chapter 54). Both were, in effect, Miss Havisham's husbands (Compeyson wooed and left her; Magwitch supplied her with a child). Pip now has to focus these two images as Wemmick has learned to focus his dual image of himself. Pip's narrating mind still delays, however, like Hamlet's. Preparations are finalized for the death journey down the Thames (Magwitch is to board the Hamburg steamer 'certainly well beyond Gravesend'; chapter 52), but the journey itself is deferred by Compeyson's note demanding his presence at the sluice-house by the limekiln. Magwitch and Compeyson can confront each other, then, only after Pip has faced his mirrored self in Orlick (chapter 53; note how the question of identity is raised in the form of Pip's uncertainty after receiving the letter: 'I was the only inside passenger, jolting away knee-deep in straw, when I came to myself. For, I really had not been myself since the receipt of the letter').

The intensity of Pip's experience as he meets Orlick is conveyed by the baptismal symbolism of the inn room in which he dines (see pp. 43–4 above): Pip is undertaking a dreamlike rite of passage in the gap between his mother's lingering death by fire and his father's last journey (chapter 54) in the form of a dying into life, a secularized version of baptism through which his dismembered self will be reassembled into psychological wholeness. Hence Pip passes by a stone quarry which 'had been worked that day, as I saw by the tools and barrows that were lying about' – image of the grave he is about to find himself on the brink of, and a bleak echo of the graveyard of *Hamlet*, V. i. He encounters the ghostly kiln vapour;

then enters the sluice-house and is caught in a noose by Orlick, bound literally now to hear that it was he who killed his sister and to realize that he is about to die, like Old Hamlet, with all his crimes upon him. Then Pip, who will recall Hamlet when he envisages himself dissolving into the vapour (see pp. 79–80 above), remembers Hamlet's own dying words as he foresees the consequences of his death at this moment:

> The death close before me was terrible, but far more terrible than death was the dread of being misremembered after death. And so quick were my thoughts, that I saw myself despised by unborn generations . . .

Joe knew the importance of being well remembered when he composed the epitaph for his father. Pip's realization applies, therefore, not only to himself but to his parents. He has *mis*-remembered them in fantasizing into existence a mad old woman, a demon of a Compeyson, a criminal of a Magwitch. Faced with the imminence of his own death he is forced to acknowledge that certain truths about the dead, as about the living, need to be suppressed because we are all at the mercy of the subjectivity of opinion. A form of justice – albeit a crude one – is achieved by scrutinizing the life-records of the dead and perpetuating their good deeds and hearts; but the complexity of the exercise is exemplified by the fact that *Great Expectations* itself, in all its variety, is one vast epitaph.

Here, by the way of parallel, is Hamlet at the end of the play that bears his name and which began with his father beseeching him 'remember me':

> Horatio, I am dead,
> Thou livest. Report me and my cause aright
> To the unsatisfied . . .
> O God, Horatio, what a wounded name,
> Things standing thus unknown, shall I leave behind me.
> If thou didst ever hold me in thy heart,
> Absent thee from felicity awhile,
> And in this harsh world draw thy breath in pain
> To tell my story.
>
> (V. ii)

It is in order that he can act as Horatio to Magwitch, reputedly 'hardened' ever since he was a little boy, and in order that he can fulfil the same function for Miss Havisham (so that she won't die as Orlick had intended Mrs Joe to, thrown into the limekiln and burned so that not a bone or rag survived), that Pip is rescued by a sobered Trabb's boy, Herbert and Startop, who burst in as Orlick is fingering Pip's nemesis in the form of 'a stone-hammer with a long heavy handle' (reminder of his rejection of Joe, so cruelly perpetuated in Herbert's nickname for him and also a reminder of his obsession with graves and funeral masonry).

Having faced his own death around 9 p.m., Pip now proceeds to guide Magwitch on his last journey, a reversal of his return from the antipodean underworld, when the tide 'turns at nine o'clock' (end of chapter 53, beginning of chapter 54), intending, as we have seen, to place his father on the *Ham*burg steamer. The journey recapitulates many of the novel's themes, taking Pip and Magwitch past 'hammers going in ship-builders' yards'; giving Magwitch the opportunity to disappear, ghost-like, behind a screen of smoke as he dips his hand in the water and sees it as an emblem of life's inscrutability; acknowledging the moment when the two pass Gravesend; and registering the similarity of the landscape here to that of Pip's own marsh country; then affording a glimpse in the lonely darkness of a collier's galley fire, 'smoking and flaring, look[ing] like a comfortable home', with its reminiscence of the welcoming glow of the fire at the forge at the beginning; and stopping for the night at an inn called 'The Ship', the name of which reaches back to the Hulks and to shiplike Satis in chapter 8. The inn is inhabited by a 'Jack' who walks in dead men's clothes and it has two bedrooms from which 'the air [is] as carefully excluded . . . as if air were fatal to life', a feature which turns them into graves.

After the confrontation with Compeyson – during which the two boats head towards each other like an object and its image in a mirror as single aims for his double – Magwitch is taken from the water, his throat clicking as it has not done since the novel's opening: 'I heard that old sound in his throat – softened now, like all the rest of him'. *Softened* because, as I have said, Pip's memory is now softened into the gentleness that can relinquish without rancour and ill feeling; softened because it is, at last, a terminal death-rattle.

Wemmick's wedding (chapter 55) interrupts the pathos of Magwitch's trial and death (chapter 56; on the trial see stage 1, section 4 (c) above), and Magwitch's wounds release him from death by hanging if not from the ignominy, which he shares with Christ, of being branded, to the end, a criminal. Pip's prayer in the final paragraph of chapter 56 – 'O Lord, be merciful to him, a sinner!' – suggests the extent to which Pip has undertaken the task of by the dying Hamlet (the prayer comes from Luke 18:10–14. In using the words of the humble publican and addressing them to Magwitch, Pip acknowledges himself to be the sinner and in doing so he tries to ensure 'justification' for Magwitch: 'And the publican, standing afar off, would not lift up so much as his eyes unto heaven, but smote upon his breast, saying, God be merciful to me a sinner. I tell you, this man went down to his house justified rather than the other . . .').

5. Pip's Return Journey and the Two Endings
chapters 57–59

Pip's life now disintegrates into fever and hallucination in which he 'confound[s] impossible existences with [his] own identity' (chapter 57). With both parents dead – Magwitch and Miss Havisham – the fever enables him to take a journey back to his origins and to rewrite his relationship with Joe, for as he comes to himself a face keeps reappearing then stabilizes itself as Joe's. Joe, with infinitely maternal tenderness, has been his nurse and carer, as he was his protector when a child. The recognition and acceptance of him – something which Pip has refused ever since he found himself in the churchyard in chapter 1 – occurs in two stages: first, Pip's 'penitential' whisper, 'O God bless him! O God bless this gentle Christian man!'; second, a couple of pages later, Pip's imagining of himself back into childhood ('Joe wrapped me up . . . as if I were still the small helpless creature to whom he had so abundantly given of the wealth of his great nature').

Pip's illness, then, enables him to redeem his memory of Joe as, earlier, he has redeemed his memory of Magwitch. The laying aside of Magwitch, Compeyson and the rest of the phantoms permits the relinquishing of his snobbish and unworthy feelings to Joe so that he can be seen for what he has been all along: a 'gentle Christian man'. And Joe relives Pip's childhood too, remembering Mrs Joe and her Rampages, explaining his role as silent spectator, and in doing so he rephrases Jaggers's question in connection with Pip's knowledge of Estella's parentage, 'for whose sake would you reveal the secret?' For Joe asks, rhetorically, 'where is the good?' of interfering when interference would not only not achieve positive results but might even cause additional harm. Thus, through memory, and using memory to achieve catharsis, Joe also redeems the past.

As Pip recovers from his fever, however, Joe distances himself from him. 'Old Pip, old chap' becomes, within the space of a sentence, 'sir', and one night Joe goes home, leaving a letter behind him as a sign of the changes within him since the novel began. Pip follows him, intending to throw himself on Biddy's mercy and ask her to marry him. Despite his 'penitence', though, he has not learned very much after all; for he will ask for her hand only after she has 'receiv[ed him] like a forgiven child' – ominous sign of the Oedipal pressures within him all along.

Joe's disappearance in the night is a final reminder to Pip that the bond between parent and child – for he has at last learned that in his love and protectiveness Joe was his real father after all – has to alter with the times. Pip cannot get back his childhood. The fever was a gift which enabled him to recapture it in order to right his relationship with Joe, a sort of drowning-man's review of life's events. But Pip as an adult must always be separated from Joe. In marrying Biddy himself, Joe imposes closure on his own narrative and forces Pip's to remain obstinately open-ended. For Pip, in his post-romantic psychological fantasizing, insists that it is possible for an adult to *become* a child and thereby fulfil himself completely. Dickens has, however, shown us what he thinks of that idea in the shape of the grotesque Harold Skimpole in *Bleak House*, and Pip's relationship with Biddy underlines in a slightly different way the pattern of his error. Biddy, starting in the novel like Pip as 'an orphan [who] had been brought up by hand' (chapter 7), has emerged gradually as Pip's superior in status, strong-willed, proud, astute in her ear for snobbery and injustice. She has taught Pip, then heard herself patronized and condescended to by him as his acquaintance with Estella grew. Her common sense and independence – her existence, in other words, beyond the limits of Pip's fantasy as well as within it – are a last reminder of the extent of his misreading of the feminine, of the way his obsessive attachment to his mother's memory has blinded him to the possibility of an independent, intelligent, loving woman, just as his partial reading of his father's tombstone engendered Magwitch and Compeyson and blinded him to Joe.

The shock that awaits Pip, therefore, as he chases after Joe to offer himself to Biddy, is to discover the forge deserted: no fire, no hammer, no father, because the parental home cannot exist for adults. Wemmick's message 'DON'T GO HOME' at the end of chapter 44 has now become the reality of 'you can't go home'. In marginalizing Joe in his consciousness and his autobiography Pip forgot that, like Biddy, he had an independent existence. Joe proves that independence by marrying Biddy and marginalizing Pip in his turn, relegating him to the boundaries of the hearth he finds himself so unable, in the end, to leave.

So, after the wedding, Pip travels to his job in the East, returning after eleven years one 'evening in December' (the month of the novel's beginning) to the forge to peep like a ghost at Joe and Biddy and to discover himself ('I again!') in their little boy, Pip, whom he

119

promptly takes 'down to the churchyard, and set him on a certain tombstone there'. When he says to Biddy, who is nursing her baby girl, 'you must give up Pip to me, one of these days; or lend him, at all events', she gently refuses: 'no. You must marry'. She then asks if he still frets for Estella.

And that is where the problem of the two endings raises itself. For the original, unpublished ending followed straight on from this in a paragraph in which Pip meets Estella in London when he is with young Pip, then parts from her (see the Penguin edition, Appendix A for the text). The printed ending, written at the request of Edward Bulwer Lytton, the novelist and friend of Dickens, has Pip proceed to Satis, see Estella lonely amid its ruins, touch her hand and, despite Estella's assurance that they will 'continue friends apart', state that he 'saw no shadow of another parting from her'.

Dickens's manuscript memoranda for the last section of the novel make it clear that Pip's concern, both friendly and financial, for Herbert is 'the one good thing he did in his prosperity, that endures and bears good fruit'. This says evidently enough, I think, that he did not envisage Pip marrying Estella. (For a facsimile and transcript, see Harry Stone, ed. and intro., *Dickens's Working Notes for His Novels* (Chicago and London: Chicago U.P., 1987), pp. 322–3.)

The revised ending is, in fact, ambiguous. The Penguin text prints, as do many other editions, Dickens's revision of the first serialized and bound edition's 'I saw the shadow of no parting from her'. (The revision reads: 'I saw no shadow of another parting from her'.) The interpretative problem lies, of course, as it would have to in this novel of ghosts, in Dickens's placing, and our exegesis, of *shadow*, and the negative that qualifies it with the notion of parting. Does he part from her for ever or not? What is the *shadow*? The answer is both a matter of syntax and that infinitely subjective thing, one's feel for the text.

My own view of the text is, by and large, dark. I agree that the first ending was the right one in terms of Pip's psychology and the overall narrative strategy of his autobiography. I also think that the 'revised' ending tried to remain consistent with the original ending. I therefore agree with Calder, the Penguin text's editor, that with the revision of the ending requested by Bulwer Lytton, Dickens worked himself round to saying, or trying to say: 'the evening sunlight of the moment when I left Satis holding Estella's hand was so bright that it banished all shadows – even the metaphorical shadow of the parting that we were so soon (and permanently) to endure'.

To return to the beginning of chapter 59 with this in mind: although he has laid Miss Havisham, Magwitch and Compeyson to rest, and although his narrative demonstrates urbanity and a certain maturity of tone and perception, Pip has never finally made the break with, and readjustment of himself in relation to, the past that psychological maturity requires. Having discarded Miss Havisham and Magwitch he has revisited Joe and wanted to retain him in paternal bondage, then he has wanted to marry his childhood friend Biddy in an attempt to keep that part of the past at least as it was. But Biddy has changed (a key word in both endings in connection with Estella) and so has Joe. They have re-formed to create a new family, the result of a temporal and emotional process that has proceeded beyond the boundaries of Pip's limited and limiting imagination. He cannot, simply, imagine anything *beyond* himself; cannot permit others to grow and alter. And Joe and Biddy conform to Pip's imagination in this – that they have named their son after the boy who used to sit in the same place in the same chair.

But Pip performs an injustice in identifying the boy as himself, and perpetrates an outrage by taking him to the churchyard to see the gravestones and setting him up, as Magwitch had set him up, on one. He tries to break through the time warp and set the past in motion again. But Biddy prevents him. *This* Pip has parents, and is in no need of an 'uncle' or stepfather or adoptive father. Biddy's 'no' to Pip's request to have him is a polite and sensible 'keep your hands off'.

Her gentle 'you must marry' is, however, a hope against hope. A man who is that bound to his childhood image of himself and to his love for his mother and obsession with his father is psychologically likely to remain unmarried and, Dickens suggests, is better so. That way his story, born of his memories and imagination, will die with him, cannot be imposed as a burden upon the young. In removing young Pip from old Pip Biddy asserts her sense as a parent. Nothing can diminish Pip's tragedy in being born orphaned, or can fully redeem his loneliness. Estella remains a fantasy based on his ideal vision of his dead mother. She is taken from him in the original, unpublished, ending, when Pip wanders off, outcast like Cain, perpetually seeking a home he has not got and can never have. In the printed endings he meets her again to envisage 'no shadow' of a parting from her. Is not that Dickens's way of telling us that he is to be parted from her, even though the shadow of the parting is obliterated by the evening sunlight, and that he still insists on clinging

121

to her in his fantasies because she is even now the image – and bears the image – of maternal Miss Havisham? The revised ending finally got it clear, I think, despite a haze of ambiguity: 'I saw no shadow of another parting from her' means, on the level of the reading I have been giving the text, 'I did not see Miss Havisham's ghost ['another' as noun] abandoning her'. Estella is still haunted by it because Pip is. He is bound upon the wheel of the 'eternal shape' of his past (the phrase is used at the beginning of chapter 56).

Conclusion

The most astonishing and wonderful thing about Dickens is the exuberance of his imagination. He was above all, particularly in his last novels, a fantasist, and it is to this that his social-reforming and 'realistic' self were subordinated. It is, of course, possible to offer various explanations of meanings and patterns in his novels, as I have done here. My primary feeling remains, though, that *Great Expectations* is a marvellously proliferating example of the fantasy at play; that the patterns that it throws up are in a sense incidental to the anarchically creative impulse that produced them. Each time I have followed through a clue to what appears to be its logical end, I came up against the fact of the comic and dream world alogic that has much of the novel in its grip and that triumphantly defeats the critic's all-too-solemn and awakened mind.

A few examples will show what I mean. Uncle Pumblechook, if we take a sociologist's view of Pip's childhood as orphan and, at the hands of Mrs Joe, battered baby, is menacing and tyrannical, one of several men who supply the gaps left by Pip's dead father at the beginning of the novel. Pip justifiably loathes him for his unctuousness and expresses his loathing by nearly 'murdering' him with tar water. The logic that has led from the graveyard and Magwitch's frightening appearance and his demand that Pip steal 'wittles' for him, which has, in turn, induced Pip to steal brandy that he has topped up with the tar water, is ominous. But what Pip sees through the window is Pumblechook dancing like a dervish with a whooping-cough cry that, however one tries to read it, is at once supremely funny and sympathy-inducing. All of which is to say, I suppose, that Pumblechook is an essentially comic creation who, like all truly comic creations, inhabits a world that is totally 'other' than the world inhabited by moral censure. The imagination which gave him birth loves him, as it loves Orlick, slouch and kill though he may. Orlick pops up where Dickens's fantasy wills, just like one of Pumblechook's seeds that has decided to break out of its drawer of a prison and bloom. And when Pip meets him as porter at Satis and he talks about hammering on the door and mutters 'Burn me, if I know!', 'Burn me, twice over, if I can say!', and then, at the end of the novel, burgles Pumblechook's house and stuffs its owner's mouth with flowering annuals in one of the funniest revenges in any novel, we realize that on the profoundest and most important level this character, with his extraordinary Christian name Dolge, just *is* because he is, and does what he does because Dickens's writing hand was at the command of a remarkably fertile demonic fantasy which dictated Orlick to him in all his outrageous impossibility. 'Burn me' is a phrase which we can, if we like, link to Miss Havisham's death by fire and the fire at the forge, but in fact it stands above and beyond thematic considerations like any comedian's catch phrase.

Or take the example of the bed which takes possession of Pip's room at the Hummums, or the way words leap off on their own to the destruction of any attempt at coherent explanation. Pip is upset because, as he discovers from Estella, 'he calls the knaves, Jacks, this boy!'. 'Jack' having been released from Dickens's word hoard (probably, as I have suggested, from the 'Jacques' of *A Tale of Two Cities*), then, like the bed, tramps off wilfully through the novel with a life of its own. *Jagg* is a common dialect word for a Jack, and the next thing we know lawyer Jaggers has made his appearance, pompous, scented, admonitory, and not at all 'jacklike' – unless of course he is the real knave of the story, in which case he may, as a paternal authority figure, have more to do with Miss Havisham's broken heart than the narrative's surface lets on. Then what about the slouching 'Jack of the causeway' when we meet him at the pub on Magwitch's final journey down river, dressed in drowned men's clothes and primevally oozelike? Why has he got a remote double of a companion in the drunken minister of justice who wears, as Pip understands the situation with dawning horror, hanged men's clothes? He is not called 'Jack' but he is like this Jack. The Jack is also, in his affinity with ooze, like Orlick, who apparently goes around saying 'I'm *jigg*ered' all the time: 'He attached no definite meaning to the word that I am aware of, but used it, like his own pretended Christian name, to affront mankind' (chapter 17). [Jigg = Jack.]

In a way that sums up, like the shackle-bursting seeds and bulbs, the 'sense' of *Great Expectations*. It is like saying, as Estella does, that Satis is 'Greek, or Latin, or Hebrew, or all three' (chapter 8): jigger, like the novel as a whole, is what you want it to be. And so *jagger*, if we consult a dialect dictionary, turns out also to be a vagrant pedlar, a pricking goad, and tattered garments: a wandering nobody (like Pip) at the centre of the novel; a pointing, pricking admonisher of criminals and justices, who made his name as a lawyer defending Molly on a charge of murder and defeating judge and jury over the matter of lacerations on her hand caused by prickly brambles; a rag-bag of a Jagger who somehow reincarnates the bramble-torn convict Magwitch who first appears 'with an old rag tied round his head' (chapter 1) and who, by the very meanings of his vagrant, ragged name undoes Pip's pretensions to sartorial and stable gentility.

And if Jaggers's name allies him, with the apparently random associationism that we experience in dreams, with these other jack-siblings in this novel which is about having no kin and trying to repair the loss of parents and siblings, then this is paradigmatic of *Great Expectations*'s way of proceeding as a whole; for it progresses by spawning doubles, triples and multiples. In this it is at one with its century, in which speculation about the double went hand in hand with hypnotism, the vogue for Mediums (mentioned, albeit jestingly, near the beginning of the novel), and the discovery of the inner self that was supposedly revealed by phrenology. More to the point, for the Dickens who, in the autobiographical fragment, voiced particular resentment against his mother and who had an equally complex relationship with his father and found peculiar satisfaction fictionalizing himself through Oliver, David Copperfield, Esther Summerson, Pip, and many others, into the role of orphan, orphans and doubles, as Karl Miller has shown, go together. As I said earlier, to those within a family the outcast orphan, marginal and wandering, becomes an image of freedom and flight from the claustrophobia of belonging and of having no privacy. Those who are orphans themselves frequently imagine a companion in exclusion and apartness as consolation and also as validation for their condition.

From one point of view, then, *Great Expectations* is an orphan's fantasy, tracing a move not unlike Dickens's own from the outcastness of poverty to arrival in the world of the wealthy. But it does something strange with that fantasy. It undermines it from the start by trailing clues about the criminal nature of Pip's real benefactor and then confirms the truth of the clues and removes every worldly possession from Pip. We can interpret this as a comment on the vanity of human wishes in the ancient moralistic and biblical tradition; we can take a Marxist realist line on it; and we can see it as an extraordinary revelation about Dickens's feelings concerning his place as a demonic worker and performer for money and public acclaim, a symbolic admission of the unsatisfyingness of the whole experience which nevertheless he is hooked on and cannot help but celebrate. Satis House *is* Gad's Hill Place in desolate ruin, the emblem of Dickens's worldly achievements seen *sub specie aeternitatis.*

Great Expectations is a poetic fantasy about power and belonging, poverty and exclusion. It defies the laws of interpretative logic by bringing its mind-boggling energies to bear on the very fact of creation itself. Yet, of course, it tells a story and stories have, or appear to have, a meaning or meanings. They generate parallels within themselves; they demonstrate causes and effects. I have argued that many of those causes and effects *are* only apparent; that *Great Expectations* operates more on the level of a-temporal associationism induced by a fundamental obsession on Pip–Dickens's part with his orphan status. Yet it would be foolish to deny its story as a narrative sequence, and it is essential to recognize and celebrate the creative exuberance. After all, the sane centre of the novel is the forge, image of warmth and divine creativity, of hammering and shaping, which makes Joe a Vulcan and a sort of Jo(vial) thunderer. Hammer is one of the key 'demonic' words in the novel, springing, like 'jack', off into a world and life of its own. But hammering people kills them: Joe's mother and Mrs Joe both die of a hammering, and this somehow reminds us of Compeyson, the gentlemanly forger, shatterer of Miss Havisham's heart, who has no heart himself at all and who shadows Pip's, Magwitch's, and practically everybody else's life throughout *Great Expectations.*

Why is Joe doubled by the forger Compeyson? It isn't a matter of arbitrary verbal punning on *forge* but of essential linkage predicated upon binary opposition. Yet once one has said that one isn't much further forward. In this story, the critic has in the end to admit, things are because they are. Compeyson and Magwitch struggle; Miss Havisham lives in her time capsule both dead and alive and evocative of the most terrible memories of lunacy and exhumed corpses; and Jaggers proceeds on his jaggering way. If we bear this in mind, it may be possible to do some justice to the brilliance of Dickens's comic and poetic gifts. What I have said in one section of this book may have contradicted or only partly complemented what is said in another section because I have been trying to suggest possibilities for meaning rather than impose a systematic interpretation. The sum of those meanings will only begin to approach the 'meaning' of *Great Expectations* because that is essentially unknowable, and also private to each of its readers. *Great Expectations* will mean what it means to you, and that is as it should be. All I and any other critic can do in the end is say, here is this wonderful novel: I think this, this and this about it. But my own final words would be: I am dazzled by its brilliance and wish, simply, to say that I love it and enjoy it in all its moving vitality.

Appendix: Pip's Letter

Max Byrd, '"Reading" in *Great Expectations*', *Publications of the Modern Language Association of America* (*PMLA*), 91 (1976), pp. 259–65 and Murray Baumgarten, 'Calligraphy and Code: Writing in *Great Expectations*', *Dickens Studies Annual*, 11 (1983), pp. 61–72, have both suspected punning of a slightly ominous nature in the letter Pip inscribes to Joe on his slate in chapter 7. In *Fielding, Dickens, Gosse, Iris Murdoch and Oedipal Hamlet*, chapter 2, I attempted a more elaborate decoding of its hidden meanings by analogy with the textual complexities of Mrs Joe's slate-written letter at the end of chapter 16, that 'curious T' which signifies *hammer* and *Orlick*.

Pip's letter reads:

MI DEEr JO i OPE U r krWiTE wEll i OPE i sHAl soN B HABelL 4 2 TEEDge U JO AN theN wE sHOrl b sO glOdd AN wEn i M prENgTD 2 u JO woT larX AN blEvE ME iNF xn PiP.

What it reveals, among other things, beneath its endearing surface is, I think, the following: a preoccupation with Pip's ambiguous status as 'son' in connection with the loaded notion of brother Abel (i sHAl soN B HABelL); a threat (i sHAl soN . . . TEEDge U JO); the intrusion, for the first time and long before his official entry in chapter 15, of Cain-like Orlick (theN wE sHOrl b sO glOdd); the admission of the problem of conception and birth in connection with the binding that Pip's apprenticeship represents to him (wEn i M prENgTD 2 u JO: *prengtd = apprenticed* but also *impregnated*, the second meaning being reinforced by *wen*, which means *swelling*); the appearance of Pip's primal mother, Eve, who is represented in the novel, as we have seen, by Miss Havisham (AN blEvE ME); and, in conjunction with that, the appearance of taint and stain associated – even identified – with love (iNFxn = *infection* as well as *affection*).

Notes

INTRODUCTION

1

On the autobiographical aspects of *GE* see, e.g., Harry Stone, 'Fire, Hand, and Gate: Dickens's *Great Expectations*', *The Kenyon Review*, 24 (1962), pp. 662–91; L. J. Dessner notes that 'the novel is Dickens's dream' and that Pip's dream is contained within it: '*Great Expectations*: the Ghost of a Man's Own Father', *Publications of the Modern Language Association of America*, 91 (1976), pp. 436–49; p. 438. The letter to Forster about *GE* is reprinted in John Forster, *The Life of Charles Dickens*, 3 vols (London, 1872–4), vol. 3, p. 329, which remains also the single best biography of Dickens. Forster must, however, nowadays be supplemented by Edgar Johnson, *Charles Dickens: His Tragedy and Triumph*, 2 vols (London: Gollancz, 1953; 1 vol revised edn, London: Allen Lane, 1977) and Christopher Hibbert, *The Making of Charles Dickens* (1967; Penguin edn, Harmondsworth, 1983). The autobiographical fragment is preserved in Forster, *Life*, vol. 1, ch. 2 (pp. 30–50).

2

For the conditions of production of a serial novel, using *Oliver Twist* as a test case, see J. A. Bull, *The Framework of Fiction: Socio-Cultural Approaches to the Novel* (London and Basingstoke: Macmillan, 1988), ch. 5. Whipple's review is reprinted in Philip Collins, ed., *Charles Dickens: The Critical Heritage* (London: Routledge and Kegan Paul, 1971), pp. 428–30. The best account of *GE* as a novel about obsessive repetition is Peter Brooks's 'Repetition, Repression and Return: *Great Expectations* and the Study of Plot', *New Literary History*, 11 (1979–80), pp. 503–26; while the Wordsworthian influence on *GE* (the idea of the child as father of the man; the balancing in one's childhood of beauty and fear, etc.) is ably discussed by Dirk den Hartog, *Dickens and Romantic Psychology: The Self in Time in Nineteenth-Century Literature* (London and Basingstoke: Macmillan, 1987), p. 143.

STAGE 1

1

Some of the biblical implications of Magwitch have been teased out by Jane Vogel in her otherwise rather extremist *Allegory in Dickens* (University, Alabama: University of Alabama Press, 1977), ch. 4. On Magwitch's name, Joseph Gold, *Charles Dickens, Radical Moralist* (Minneapolis: University of Minneapolis Press, 1972), p. 243, notes that *mag* means, among other things, *to steal*. The Ophelia type is discussed in fascinating detail by Showalter, *The Female Malady*, ch. 3 and, in connection with *GE*, in my *Fielding, Dickens, Gosse, Iris Murdoch and Oedipal 'Hamlet'* (London and Basingstoke: Macmillan, 1989), ch. 2. Dickens's visit to the asylum, St Luke's Hospital, is recounted in 'A Curious Dance Round a Curious Tree' (17 January 1852): *Charles Dickens: Uncollected Writings from 'Household Words' 1850–1859*, ed. Harry Stone, 2 vols (Bloomington: Indiana University Press, 1968), vol. 2, pp. 387–8.

The Oedipus complex as the basis of Freud's perception of male psychology and male-female relationships is analysed in Peter Rudnytsky's superb *Freud and Oedipus* (New York: Columbia University Press, 1987). It is now critical orthodoxy to assume Oedipal underpinnings to many of Dickens's texts: e.g., Julian Moynahan, 'The Hero's Guilt: The Case of *Great Expectations*', *Essays in Criticism*, 10 (1960), pp. 60–79; Dessner, art. cit.; Dianne Sadoff, '*Locus Suspectus*: Narrative, Castration, and the Uncanny', *Dickens Studies Annual*, 13 (1984), pp. 207–29, and her 'The Dead Father: *Barnaby Rudge, David Copperfield*, and *Great Expectations*', *Papers on Language and Literature*, 18 (1982), pp. 36–57; Peter Brooks, art. cit.; Steven Connor, *Charles Dickens* (Oxford: Basil Blackwell, 1985), ch. 6 (on *GE*); and my own chapter on *GE* in *Oedipal 'Hamlet'*.

On Dickens and Maria Beadnell, see Johnson, *Charles Dickens*, 1-vol. edn, ch. 5, and Hibbert, *The Making of Charles Dickens*, ch. 5. For Dickens's burning of his papers, see Johnson, ch. 42.

Bert G. Hornback notices the fallen, post-Edenic, quality of *GE*'s landscapes in *'Noah's Arkitecture': A Study of Dickens's Mythology* (Athens, Ohio: Ohio University Press, 1972), pp. 130–31, as does Vogel, *Allegory in Dickens*, ch. 4. Miss Havisham's name is usually interpreted, rather weakly, as Have-a-sham, supposedly in allusion to false appearances at Satis (Stone, 'Fire, Hand, and Gate', p. 677).

However, it is worth noting that as a verb *haver = to speak gibberish*, which reirforces the notion of Miss Havisham as lunatic.

2

The Darwinian background is described best by Gillian Beer, *Darwin's Plots: Evolutionary Narrative in Darwin, George Eliot, and Nineteenth-Century Fiction* (London: Routledge and Kegan Paul, 1983), and see p. 63 for the relevant perception that Darwin's theory 'muddied descent' by making us all members of an extended family which would never permit the aspiring social climber to forget his lowly origins. The word, and idea, of *struggle* was privileged by the full title of Darwin's treatise: *The Origin of Species by Means of Natural Selection or the Preservation of Favoured Races in the Struggle for Life*.

On Compeyson's name as *compaysan*, see E. L. Gilbert, '"In Primal Sympathy": *Great Expectations* and the Secret Life', *Dickens Studies Annual*, 11 (1983), pp. 89–113, and on Orlick as double, Moynahan, 'The Hero's Guilt', and Stone, 'Fire, Hand, and Gate', pp. 666ff. The complexities of Estella as forbidden and forbidding yet seductively attractive object of desire are provocatively discussed by Graham Daldry, *Charles Dickens and the Form of the Novel: Fiction and Narrative in Dickens's Work* (London and Sydney: Croom Helm, 1987), ch. 5; J. O. Jordan, 'The Medium of *Great Expectations*', *Dickens Studies Annual*, 11 (1983), pp. 73–88; and Peter Brooks, art. cit., pp. 515–16. Dianne Sadoff, '*Locus Suspectus*', is good on Dickens's 'phallic mothers'.

Orlick and Drummle: the connection between the two is confirmed by Drummle's name. It is a form of *drumble* which, as a verb, means *to make water muddy* and as a substantive means *mud*. As an adjective it also means *stupid, dull-witted*; see the *English Dialect Dictionary*, s.v. drumble.

3

Recommended *Barnwell* text: George Lillo, *The London Merchant*, ed. W. H. McBurney, Regents Restoration Drama Series (London: Edward Arnold, 1965). For suggestive comments on Barnwell and Pip see, most recently, Eiichi Hara, 'Stories Present and Absent in *Great Expectations*', *ELH: A Journal of English Literary History*, 53 (1986), pp. 593–613, esp. pp. 597–600.

4 (a)

On the meaning of Adam's name see, e.g., John Robinson, *A Theological, Biblical, and Ecclesiastical Dictionary* (London, 1815), s.v. Adam: 'ADAM . . . signifies *earthly man, red, of the colour of blood*': and for Dickens's fascination with hanging and the facts surrounding it, Philip Collins, *Dickens and Crime* (London: Macmillan, 1962), ch. 10.

(b)

The heart as a 'mystic entity' and repository of right feelings for Dickens is discussed fully in M. S. Kearns, 'Associationism, the Heart, and the Life of the Mind in Dickens's Novels', *Dickens Studies Annual*, 15 (1986), pp. 111–44. Collins, *Dickens and Crime*, p. 5, observes on the evidence of the *Oxford English Dictionary* that 'penology' was invented as a word in 1838 in America.

(c)

On Hulks see also Collins, pp. 5–7.

(d)

Denis Walder, *Dickens and Religion* (London: Allen and Unwin, 1981), pp. 200–201, having noted that *GE* has as its underlying *schema* 'the familiar . . . pattern of sin, repentance and regeneration', comments aptly that the novel opens with 'a Christmas for the fallen'.

5

Memory: Andrew Sanders, *Charles Dickens: Resurrectionist* (London and Basingstoke: Macmillan, 1982), p. 33, suggests the extent to which memory for Dickens supplied immortality.

For the stranger and the file, Steven Connor, *Charles Dickens*, ch. 6, is good, if eccentric on phallic and other sexual symbolisms in the novel. On Hermes-Mercury, consult any decent mythological handbook (e.g., Robert Graves, *The Greek Myths*, 2 vols (Harmondsworth: Penguin, 1977)). Frank Kermode's comments on the 'hermetic stranger' in Henry Green's novel *Party Going* are also pertinent: *The Genesis of Secrecy* (Cambridge, Mass. and London, 1979), pp. 6–8.

Pumblechook and Hades: Hades, as lord of the underworld, is traditionally guardian of dormant seeds, particularly in his role of ravisher into the underworld of Persephone, daughter of the corn mother Demeter: e.g., Andrew Tooke, *The Pantheon* (London, 1824), Part 4, ch. 2.

Trabb's boy as double: on this and other doubles, see K. P. Wentersdorf, 'Mirror Images in *Great Expectations*', *Nineteenth-Century Fiction*, 21 (1966–7), pp. 203–24.

STAGE 2

1

On Dickens and the city, see Alexander Welsh, *The City of Dickens* (Oxford: Clarendon Press, 1971) and F. S. Schwarzbach, *Dickens and the City* (London: Athlone Press, 1979).

Magwitch's clicking throat: this is mechanical, too, as Dorothy Van Ghent noticed in what is still one of the best essays on the novel in her *The English Novel: Form and Function* (New York: Harper Torchbooks, 1961), p. 130, relating it to the contemporary preoccupation with and exploitation of mechanization and the consequent de-animation of human beings. William Oddie notes how Dickens was influenced by Carlyle's attack on mechanism and the 'clockwork universe' in *Dickens and Carlyle: The Question of Influence* (London: Centenary Press, 1972), p. 65.

2

Wemmick's mourning jewellery conforms to nineteenth-century norms: Philippe Ariès, *Images of Man and Death*, tr. Janet Lloyd (Cambridge, Mass. and London: Harvard University Press, 1985), colour plate 7 and monochrome plates 352 and 390.

Gallows, *A Tale of Two Cities*, and *GE*: in many ways, not least the idea of the double, the hammer symbol, the return of the dead, and the irruption of the revolutionary mob (as Magwitch irrupts into *GE*), *GE* is a transposition of *A Tale* into a more psychologically introspective key. Among those who have commented on the parallels are: Oddie, *Dickens and Carlyle*, pp. 63 ff., and J. H. Hagen, Jr, 'The Poor Labyrinth: The Theme of Social Injustice in Dickens's *Great Expectations*', *Nineteenth-Century Fiction*, 9 (1954–5), pp. 169–78, esp. pp. 176–7. Even the door to Tellson's bank has a 'weak rattle in its throat': *Tale*, Part 2, ch. 12.

3

Primal scene: for Freud, this was the very young child's viewing of his parents in the act of sexual intercourse: e.g., Peter Rudnytsky, *Freud and Oedipus*, pp. 71–5.

4

On Herbert's family as 'but one of the novel's subsidiary families through whom Pip's psychic history is recalled and obliquely expressed', see L. J. Dessner, '*Great Expectations*: "the Ghost of a Man's Own Father"', p. 440.

5

Hall of mirrors: Steven Connor is excellent on mirrors, narcissism, reflexivity, and the idea of looking: see his chapter on *GE* in his *Charles Dickens*, pp. 126–37.

Geoffrey Hill: the title of his recent collection of essays is *The Lords of Limit: Essays on Literature and Ideas* (London: André Deutsch, 1984).

The oppressed Molly: Fred Kaplan notes that Jaggers has a mesmeric control over her in *Dickens and Mesmerism* (Princeton: Princeton University Press, 1975), p. 176. Jaggers has, of course, a considerable part to play in the novel's sexual, and other, power politics.

6

Pepper: as a verb, it means 'to inflict severe punishment or suffering upon' (*OED*, Pepper, verb, 5).

7

Hamlet: for an extended reading of the relationship between *GE* and the play, see ch. 2 of my *Oedipal 'Hamlet'*; also, W. A. Wilson, 'The Magic Circle of Genius: Dickens' Translations of Shakespearean Drama in *Great Expectations*', *Nineteenth-Century Fiction*, 40 (1985), pp. 154–74. My quotations from *Hamlet* are from the Arden edition by Harold Jenkins (London and New York: Methuen, 1982).

8

Stock and stone: Peter Brooks, 'Repetition, Repression, and Return', p. 514, notes that 'the Eastern story' which ends ch. 38 and thus heralds Magwitch's return suggests 'punishment for erotic transgression'. What we should further note is that the punishment takes the form of the collapse of the ceiling when a slab of stone falls on the bed as the retaining rope is severed. The stone causes burial, turning the bed into a closed grave; while the rope hints at hanging once more.

9

Sydney Carton's death is brilliantly analysed in terms of drowning by Garrett Stewart, 'The Secret Life of Death in Dickens', *Dickens Studies Annual*, 11 (1983), pp. 177–207.

Magwitch's sea journey: J. A. Hynes notices a parallel with the sufferings of St Paul in II Corinthians 11:25–6: 'Image and Symbol in *Great Expectations*', ELH: A Journal of English Literary History, 30 (1963), pp. 258–92, pp. 260–61.

The Ghost and the Revolution: thus confirming the connections noted earlier between Magwitch and the Revolution recorded in horrified detail in *A Tale of Two Cities*.

STAGE 3

1

Frankenstein: among the critics who have commented on *Frankenstein*'s impact on *GE*, special mention should be made of J. Hillis Miller, *Charles Dickens: The World of His Novels* (Bloomington and London: Indiana University Press, 1973), p. 273.

2

Waking into being in *Paradise Lost*: see Eve's account in Book 4 and Adam's dream in Book 8.

Christianity in *GE*: the novel, with its complex internal logic, registers more than a degree of unease with Christianity, expressing a sceptical radicalism Dickens would not have espoused so readily in a non-fictional work. On Dickens's avowed commitment to Christianity, see Dennis Walder, *Dickens and Religion*.

Orlick, Old Nick, the sluice-house: Harry Stone, 'Fire, Hand, and Gate', p. 672, notes that in going to the sluice-house Pip is journeying to the underworld and encountering the devil.

4

Pantomime: Pip may even have his origin in a similar burletta by H. J. Byron, *The Maid and the Magpie* (1858), in which the hero Pippo expresses his wish to act the role of Hamlet: Stanley Friedman, 'The Complex Origins of Pip and Magwitch', *Dickens Studies Annual*, 15 (1986), pp. 221–31; and for the Union Jack's benedictory role in an almost identical entertainment, *Bleak House*, ch. 21.

5

The two endings: 'I saw no shadow of another parting from her' dates from the Library edition of 1862. For a full discussion see Edgar Rosenberg, 'Last Words on *Great Expectations*: A Textual Brief of the Six Endings', *Dickens Studies Annual*, 9 (1981), pp. 87–115. See also M. W. Gregory, 'Values and Meanings in *Great Expectations*: The Two Endings Revisited', *Essays in Criticism*, 19 (1969), pp. 402–9; Martin Meisel, 'The Ending of *Great Expectations*', Essays in Criticism, 15 (1965), pp. 326–31; and Milton Millhauser, '*Great Expectations*: The Three Endings', *Dickens Studies Annual*, 2 (1972), pp. 267–77.